W9-BOL-889

DESTINY
VALLEY

DESTINY VALLEY

A Western Story

FRED GROVE

Five Star
Unity, Maine

Five Star First Edition Western Series.

First Edition, Second Printing

Published in 2000 in conjunction with
Golden West Literary Agency.

Set in 11 pt. Plantin by Al Chase.

Printed in the United States on permanent paper.

Library of Congress Cataloging-in-Publication Data

Grove, Fred.
   Destiny Valley : a novel / by Fred Grove.
     p.   cm.
   ISBN 0-7862-2116-X (hc : alk. paper)
   1. New Mexico — Fiction. I. Title.
  PS3557.R7 D47 2000
  813′.54—dc21   00-044270

DESTINY
VALLEY

Chapter One

He had not coughed blood now for six months and twenty straight days, and a growing awareness that somehow he had been spared and was going to be himself again, or nearly so, filled him with boundless gratitude, here in this humble cabin in the great Gila Wilderness of New Mexico Territory. Each day he awoke with the old fear. Morning was always muster time, coughing into a piece of cloth or a bandanna, hoping against hope that he'd see no reddish film accompanied by that telltale twinge in his left lung. Every free day he marked on a tablet.

In his wishful desire to live during these two and a half years since the Civil War's end, he had found only bitter disappointment: in Florida, in the mountains of North Carolina, in Canada, and in the Catskills. He'd liked the Catskills very much, hated to leave them. Maybe it had been the altitude. Buttressed by hope, he would feel better at each place for a short while, gaining appetite and strength, then the yellow phlegm with bleeding would start over again. He didn't understand why. The doctors did but avoided telling him to his face. But he could tell by their downcast silence that they had given up on him. He was, in the common parlance of the times, a lunger without hope.

As a consequence, he had given up hope, gone to the home of his anxious parents in Philadelphia to spend his last days, careful to seclude himself as much as possible to avoid infecting loved ones, facing up to his finality. He could accept that after what he had witnessed many times in bloody Virginia. One dreary afternoon at home, while morosely browsing through a clutter of miscellany in his trunk, he had come across a diary he'd kept off and on while stationed at Fort Craig in 1858 on the west side of the Río Grande. Then Second Lieutenant Evan H. Shelby, sir, 4th cavalry, a proud and very correct shavetail fresh out of West Point. The post was located on a mesa overlooking the northern stretch of the Jornado del Muerto—Dead Man's Journey—an important trade and communications route between northern and southern New Mexico. One of its primary missions had been to protect travelers along the trail from Apaches. *When we could catch them,* he smiled wryly. It was while chasing an especially elusive Apache called Chato that he had discovered the Gila Wilderness, far to the southwest.

With a sudden awakening, he reread his scrawled words, written by the light of a campfire. **Today we rode into a region I'd never seen before. Towering, majestic pines, crystal-clear streams singing their happy songs, and the purest air I'd ever breathed. Bracing and pine-scented. So clean. I want to come back here someday.**

They hadn't caught Chato, but at least they had chased him away from the settlements along the Río Grande.

Three days after reading his diary, he had boarded a train going west, his destiny like a map in his mind. Once again leaving teary, ever-hopeful parents. In El Paso he had caught a stage to Mesilla, New Mexico. There another stage had taken him, northwest, the distant promise of the mountains before him, up the cheerful Mimbres River to a little village called Rosita.

Now, reclining here on a crude bunk with a mattress of pine boughs, listening to early morning bird song, he let his eyes stray over the one room, enjoying these moments before rising. His few books and newspapers stacked on a board nailed crosswise to corner logs. Very fancy. Hanging over there his captain's uniform with twin bars. At hand his seven-shot Spencer carbine and Colt Army .44 revolver. Old cautions from the past had prompted him to bring his weapons. This part of New Mexico was still Apache frontier, although quiet at present, which meant maybe so, maybe not. But why bring his uniform? Why hadn't he left it with his proud parents? Why bring it? One thing, it was a link to better times, before he was stricken, when he was looking forward to the war's end, of going back into civilian life as editor of his father's weekly *Gazette*, or staying in the Army, to be posted out West again. He liked New Mexico; it grew on a man. He hadn't decided. It was good then to have a choice.

He had begun to feel extremely worn, with little appetite, and had started coughing the last three months of the fighting around Petersburg: likely hastened by incessant rain and mud and wet chills, horrible sanitation and bad drinking water. Others also were coughing. Soon after Appomattox an Army doctor had sadly informed him that he had contracted tuberculosis. He'd survived a dozen or more engagements, including the classic back-and-forth bloodletting at Brandy Station, only to get this fatal word. He'd never heard of anyone recovering from the dread disease. His paternal grandmother had died of it. He wondered if he had inherited a family weakness. Stunned, he had requested and been granted an immediate medical discharge and then bade his shocked friends farewell.

Now, covering blankets aside, he rose and went to the cabin door, slid back the bar, opened the door, and inhaled deeply of the God-blessed, pine-scented, healing air for long moments. Then he cleared his throat and coughed into a blue bandana, lightly, now heavily, not daring to fool himself. *He had to know every morning.* Seeing no bloody film, not the faintest trace, and the mucous light and clear, feeling no

9

sharp pain in his lung, he bowed his head and offered a fervent prayer of gratitude. After all these months, it occurred to him it was about time to cease keeping daily count. But he gloried in each clear start of a day; he wouldn't stop yet. In truth, he was afraid to. The longest he'd gone before coming to New Mexico was fifteen days in the Catskills. Just when he'd begun to feel that he might be on the road to good health again, the bleeding had returned, a grim reminder that he was eventually doomed. The setback had crushed him, broken his spirit, and he'd gone home to die. Here, he could only wonder why he'd been spared this long. Was it merely a teasing respite, only a temporary suspension of his death sentence? Was the good air alone the reason he'd come this far? Well, after what he'd been through, he was not about to question his deliverance. He would thank God with all his heart each morning and say no more.

It was still early spring, the mornings still crisp, so he set about at once building a cheerful fire in the squat little stove, and shortly the sweet smell of crackling juniper spread over the room. Then he filled the coffee pot with water from the cedar bucket and ground coffee for the pot, indulging his cavalryman's fetish for strong brew.

But a man wasn't worth a damn if he fed himself before he fed his horse. He strode to the pole corral behind the cabin and led the short-backed, dark bay gelding to the noisy stream. He called the horse Dan, after a reliable Morgan that had carried him through the last two years of the war. Coming back to the half-shed he used for a stable, he took a can and dipped oats from a crude wooden bin into the feedbox and threw down hay from the loft, which he had constructed at the other end of the shed. At least, the shed, although open on one side, was shelter enough in a storm. In fact, he was somewhat proud of having erected shed and bin by himself. The corral, apparently of later vintage than the cabin, had required only some new poles and additional support. All this he had accomplished at a leisurely pace, carefully rationing his strength for fear he might start up the bleeding again. That he had not gave him added hope and confidence in what he could do as a man.

He sat down to a breakfast of strong coffee, thick bacon, two eggs scrambled with green chilies, two fat sourdough biscuits left over from yesterday's big batch, followed by a dish of dried apricots from the valley sweetened with a little sugar. He was getting rather good at biscuits, to the extent of proudly mailing home his recipe, which he said had never failed. He had developed a hearty appetite here, gaining weight and strength, in contrast to his old malaise and alarming thinness. They said his dear grandmother, suffering with hacking spasms of coughing, had wasted away until she was mere skin and bones and continually beseeched the good Lord to take her away, which He did.

He now enjoyed a variety of good food. Now and then the Garzas, Pablo and Josefa, brought him eggs and tortillas, dried chiles and dried fruit, and jerked deer. There was an informal agreement between them for such needs, but he virtually had to force payment on them each time; furthermore, they always brought heaping amounts.

"*Señor* Evan, you pay too much," Pablo would protest, and Evan would laugh and reply: "Far from it. I don't pay you enough. You and Josefa are most generous, and it's at least five miles up here from your place." Josefa, plump, always smiling, rode their lone mule, while Pablo walked, wiry and tireless.

Evan had become acquainted with them when inquiring in the village for a woodcutter. Pablo not only cut wood. To support their growing black-eyed brood, he raised and sold chickens and eggs, irrigated a large vegetable garden and or-chard, hunted deer, did leather work and carpentry, ran a few head of cattle, and at times was called on as a freighter.

For other supplies, mail, and newspapers, Evan rode into town once a week. The obliging proprietor of the livery barn and wagon yard, Silas Brown, delivered forage at reasonable prices. Evan's gelding had come from Brown's corral of saddle horses and wagon and buggy stock.

Evan always insisted the Garzas have coffee with him and tell him any news. As a safeguard, he washed everything in hot, soapy water, and afterward rinsed in more hot water from the tea kettle. Seeing them was a break in his solitary ex-istence, a social visit, really. He appreciated these warm-hearted, hard-working people, whom he also regarded as good friends, and sensed they harbored the same feeling for him. Now that he was feeling so well, reason reminded him that he should tell them, henceforth, he should ride to their farm and save them the uphill trip. Yet, he decided, today wasn't the time. They enjoyed coming here. It pleased him to think that he might be friendlier to Mexicans than some Anglos he'd seen.

On departing last time, Josefa as usual had urged him to take care of himself, and as a postscript: "You must eat more chee-lehs. They will make you *muy* strong."

He had promised so readily, she and Pablo laughed at him.

On this day, after breakfast, he took the Spencer and went for his daily walk through the forest, a distance of about three miles. Higher up was bear country, but he had no hankering to shoot one and memorialize the event by carving his name and date on a tree, which he'd read as a boy that dauntless Daniel Boone had done. Furthermore, he'd heard bear meat was greasy. Chancing upon one months ago, while it dug grubs under a log, he had shown the good sense to overcome his curiosity and retreat as rapidly as possible. On the way today, he paused twice to rest briefly and enjoy the pristine surroundings. *Three months ago,* he mused, *I would have stopped to rest four times.* He had come to believe that the high, dry climate gave a man added strength, cleaned out his lungs, and the winter snows spent in a snug cabin had likewise contributed a particular zest. He paused again, thankful for all things.

At the cabin he changed into boots and dressed for town. Glancing into the hanging hand mirror, he saw a somewhat angular face with wide-set brown eyes and an even-lipped mouth, framed by a dark-brown beard he kept trimmed. His face was filling out. Six months ago it was drawn and haggard, the look of despair there. Now there was hope and a sense of well-being.

With quickness in his step, he left the cabin and saddled the restless bay, mounted, and struck out for Rosita, the Spencer riding in a cavalry boot under his right leg. He'd left the revolver behind. From long familiarity, he somehow felt more at ease with the carbine. No man went unarmed, even in peaceful times. Some distance on he drew rein to enjoy the gentle sweep of the Mimbres River, like a ribbon of silver, the lifeblood of the valley. It came singing out of the pristine Black Range, to Evan, a happy stream.

Humble adobes and a few taller log buildings comprised the village of Rosita, lolling under lofty cottonwoods along the west flank of the river. The spire of the Catholic Church rose above all, a benign eye overlooking the tranquil countryside. Huddled within its shadow a one-room schoolhouse. He thought of the hardy people, mostly Mexicans, like the Garzas, who tilled the little farms up and down the river. Some Anglos and Mexicans operated small ranches that ranged into the mountains. No big outfits had moved in yet.

Rather, he corrected himself, no big outfits had yet discovered the valley, protected by its isolation. He knew everything changed in time. Someday timber barons might come. Trappers, working the streams in the early days, had left few traces. There were still beaver in the upper streams. His own cabin, its roof fallen in when he'd found it, had once sheltered trappers.

Rosita was so small and its environs generally so quiet it had need of only a part-time marshal, the obliging Silas Brown. Jail was a pine tree to which infrequent prisoners were chained. Threat of such public ignominy alone was often enough to settle matters quickly, before they reached Justice of Peace Court at the general store. Of course, fights occurred at country dances over affairs of the heart, and there had been occasional shootings over livestock. In that event, but without a fatality, the guilty party usually left the valley until the issue cooled off, probably for always-safe Mexico, where no questions were asked, or he rode to Arizona, where big cow outfits needed riders.

The proximity of Fort Bayard, west over the mountains, and Fort Cummings, just beyond the southern tip of the Mimbres Mountains at Cooke's Spring, gave Rosita a measure of protection from Apache raids. The last attack, two years ago, from the north, had been a quick-hitting grab for horses and mules. A cavalry detachment from Fort Bayard failed to catch the invaders, echoes of the elusive Chato; Evan had smiled when told about it at the store. Trouble was, Rosita and the post lacked a linking telegraph line for quick response. By the time the troopers gave chase, the trail was more than a day old.

Riding on, he halted at the river running clear and strong. While his horse drank, he listened to the Mimbres murmuring its *sh-sh-sh*. An ever-present breeze through here made the cottonwood leaves shake like spangles.

An abrupt sound interrupted his musing—trotting horses. Across the river two riders appeared headed for the village, one leading a pack mule. The riders wore wide-brimmed hats pulled low. They seemed to ride with a purpose. Their mounts looked hard-used, as if they had come a long way. The pair gave him a quick, hard glance. Valley men would have waved, whether they recognized him or not.

Leisurely he forded the river and turned toward Rosita. Before long he caught the faint hum of voices and the busy clanging of the blacksmith shop. It was good to hear voices. He missed people, but that was part of the price a man paid in his position, and which he did not complain about one bit. He was lucky to be alive. He always looked forward to coming here. *There isn't one unfriendly face,* he thought, jogging into town.

Across the street from the general store, Hannah Young was making dust fly as she swept the verandah of the Mimbres Hotel, a two-story log structure with a small restaurant and six rooms upstairs. It was clean, and the food, a generous mixture of Anglo and Mexican, was quite good. Her coffee would straighten a man up in the morning. Evan had stayed there some days while he looked for a permanent place to live. Mrs. Young, a stout, plain-faced, no-foolishness yet pleasant ranch widow past middle age, owned and managed the hotel. No drunken cowboys allowed. No sneaking Mexican girls upstairs. Although there was also a rear entrance, for reasons of fire safety, it was said no couple had managed to beat her surveillance. Poker was permitted, if played quietly; as a result, there was none, and all gambling took place across the street in the raucous Gem Saloon.

"One day a fancy woman from El Paso stepped off the stage," Evan recalled her telling him. "I think she was scoutin' out the Mimbres, lookin' for new territory. It was afternoon, and the Gem was noisy as usual. Some of the cowboys were whooping it up a little. She couldn't miss hearing 'em, and I caught the look in her eyes. Little Rosita was like a bird nest on the ground, ready for the takin'. I invited her in and said enjoy our wonderful climate, but informed her there wasn't gonna be any monkey business in my hotel. . . . She caught the next stage back. The wait bored her almost to tears."

After waving at Hannah, he tied up at the store, which also housed the U.S. Post Office, that received mail off the weekly stages from east and west. The Gem was next door. A barbershop and saddlery filled out that side of the street between the store and the livery. Evan noticed more than the usual number of horses lined up at the Gem hitching track. Booted men passed in and out of the saloon and others occupied benches on the boardwalk in front of the store and the Gem, smoking and talking. He wondered about these men and why they were here, as he thought one would at sight of strangers in a small town or village. From newspaper accounts he understood there was considerable shifting about across much of the nation, North and South. The war-torn South was short of capital, and veterans on both sides needed jobs. Out West a man could go where he pleased in search of better prospects, if he could handle the challenge, himself included.

He entered the store. William J. Keeley was both store owner and postmaster, and also Justice of the Peace, and owned the Gem, which Cap Shaw ran for him. A back room of the store served as an undertaking parlor for the entire valley. Keeley had brought in an elderly Mexican as the mortician. Short and thick-set, with a large head of white curly hair and a close-cropped beard, Keeley always seemed to be in control of himself and all around him, filling his many rôles.

He started shaking hands ten feet away when he saw Evan, who sensed that a keen mind went with Keeley's cordial greeting. A proclaimed Democrat, he was said to have political and business connections far beyond Rosita that extended to the capital at Santa Fé and down to Las Cruces for trade and banking purposes. It might be said, he was Rosita.

"How are you, Captain?" Keeley asked.

"Couldn't be better, sir. Thank you. And you this good day?"

"Fine. Mighty fine."

"Do I have any mail?"

"Yes, indeed. A letter and some Sunday newspapers from back East." He turned to his makeshift post office, a cupboard affair with boxes for letters, and, when Evan went to the counter, Keeley handed him a bundle of newspapers with the letter. The letter was from his dear mother, which he opened at once. A distant uncle in Ohio had passed away. His biscuit recipe was very good, except for one thing: it made too many. So she had cut it in half. Could he come home sometime for a visit? Yes, he'd write them, when he was certain he had fully recovered. Better wait a while yet. Right now he was feeling fine. He wished he could think of something to send them; at least, he wrote regularly. Rosita had no curio shop. No local objects of art.

His mother wrote that Marian Clark, who had married Cletus Dodson, now had their third child, another boy. Cletus, Evan recalled, had served in the artillery; invalided out early, he had gone into the hardware business with his father. Evan remembered Marian as the prettiest girl in school. A fine girl. He had dated her a few times when he came home on furlough from West Point. Both families had beamingly approved. But there had been no actual romance. He and Marian were just good friends, his date at parties. He

17

wished her and Cletus happiness. At the Point some of his classmates had married upon graduating. Although he had enjoyed the company of more than one much-admired girl, he hadn't found one to pursue with serious intent. At Fort Craig it was mostly a bachelor's existence, and, when he learned he had contracted the fatal disease in 1865, he was thankful he had no immediate family to leave in dire straits and mourn his passing, or he to mourn losing them. Still, a man's life was incomplete without a family. Someday. . . .

Gathering up his newspapers, he nodded at Keeley and commented: "I see Rosita has visitors."

Keeley shrugged. "Appears they'll be here a while," and offered no more. The storekeeper was always tactful for business reasons.

As Evan walked out, he saw a man standing by his mount, staring at his sheathed carbine. Now the man put a hand on the protruding stock of the Spencer. Evan moved faster. The man was about to draw the carbine when Evan said: "Hold on, there."

The other let go and faced about. "Jest aimed to look at it."

"Usually," Evan said, taken aback by the boldness, "you ask a man's permission to look at his weapon."

In return, Evan got a bold sizing-up. A kind of glittery appraisal crept into the light-colored eyes under the wide-brimmed hat worn low, in the pinched face with a grayish beard. A hard-times face.

"What would you do if I grabbed the carbine?" the man challenged.

"I'd break your arm," Evan assured him, sensing that they had drawn an audience. Something about this man seemed vaguely familiar. Not as an individual, but somehow as a group.

Now the man made a sudden, teasing move toward the carbine.

Evan didn't go for it, saying: "Don't try it."

"Let it alone, Code," an authoritative voice called from in front of the saloon. "You're delaying the gentleman."

Code's manner changed at once. "I jest wanted to look at it," he answered. And to Evan: "I reckon it is a Spencer?"

"It is," Evan said.

"I remember these little short-barreled killers in Tennessee. Jest kept a-shootin'."

"Seven rounds in the magazine," Evan explained. "An eight-shooter with one in the chamber." He placed the man now. He reminded Evan of prisoners taken around Petersburg during the final days, when the Confederacy was crumbling and Rebs, lean and hungry, without rations for days, began surrendering.

"Reckon you know, Yank," Code said.

"I also reckon that Reb muzzleloaders were damned effective up to a thousand yards," Evan said to even up matters.

Code crimped his mouth in a thin way, and Evan stuffed his mail into a saddlebag, mounted, and rode down the street, puzzled at what had occurred back there. One wrong word or move would have set off a fight. Code also packed a handgun. The war wasn't over yet; it would gnaw at men's guts for a generation or more. Furthermore, Evan felt certain, the man called Code would have taken the Spencer had he not stopped him. Evan would have fought him. It angered him to think about it. Steal a man's carbine in broad daylight! If Evan had been a minute later leaving the store, Code could have hidden the carbine. Another thought: would the authoritative man have ordered Code to return it?

After this, if these riders hung around town, he would be wise to pack his Colt, leave the Spencer at the cabin or take it

Fred Grove

inside the store. Who were these people, anyway? Why had they come to peaceful Rosita?

Jim "Bear" Webb rested on his customary rawhide-covered chair in front of **Silas Brown's Acme Livery**, taking in the sun. Next door was **Brown's Wagon Yard,** and next to it the clanging blacksmith shop, so said a faded sign in front. Evan pulled up and dismounted.

A once-powerful man reduced to a shadow of himself by the claws of a grizzly, yet insisting he be called Bear, Webb cocked the one good eye in his disfigured face and said: "Couldn't hear, but I saw enough. But you backed him down. A wonder he didn't ride off on your horse. Things are changin' fast. Look yonder," he said, inclining his head.

Across the street an Anglo was putting up a sign on an adobe. The sign read: **Land Office**.

"Two lawyer-lookin' *hombres* got off the El Paso stage yesterday. They talked to Silas this mornin' about rentin' saddle horses or a rig."

"Who's behind this, Bear? What is it?"

"It'll all float to the surface at the Gem before long, when the whisky fumes get strong enough. Count on it. Silas will hear when he goes for his mornin' phlegm-cutter."

"I believe that's a solid prediction," Evan said, with a grin. "You take care of yourself now, Bear."

"Same to you, Cap'n. You're lookin' better all the time."

Evan mounted and rode on down the street. He didn't mind that he was known as a lunger. It was not a disgrace. Before long, with good luck, he would be a walking example of how the valley and mountains could make a man well again. Turning his mind to the land office, he reasoned that meant ranching or mining. There could be no other purposes.

Dr. R.W. Renshaw, himself once a lunger, had come West

for his health twenty years ago from Indiana. The valley's lone practitioner, he always seemed a little tired. A manner of endless patience offset his worn appearance. He seldom hurried. A tall, lank-bodied man with grayish-blue eyes and a shock of gray hair cropped short, he looked almost hulking and awkward. His large hands possessed a kindly touch, and his voice matched his hands. The Mexicans loved him, often brought him produce from their gardens and orchards. Unmarried, he lived behind his office, and a Mexican woman cooked his meals. A small adobe next door served as an infirmary. He made his rounds in a buggy drawn by a plodding trotter known as Amos.

Once a month Evan came in for an examination. A consultative talk, fatherly in tone, always followed.

"I think you're over the hump," Renshaw said. "Provided you continue to look out for yourself. You have a strong constitution. Give yourself a year to be sure. Continue plenty of rest and good food, and moderate exercise. No undue straining." A smile broke through his fatigue. "Such as moving boulders. You'd be surprised what some men try to do when they get to feeling better. As if they have to prove something. Also, no heavy drinking . . . a case in point, myself. Years ago I got to feeling good and went on a week's spree. In my younger days I liked the taste of whisky. Well, I started coughing again. Scared the hell out of me, back to common sense." He let his understanding settle on Evan before he spoke again. "I don't mean you can't have a drink. You can now and then . . . better to weaken it with water. But, absolutely, no sprees."

"I've been afraid to drink anything but water and coffee. However, I do enjoy the taste of Kentucky bourbon. But I've never been a heavy drinker."

"Have a drink once in a while, if you want it. A beer would

21

be all right . . . even better. I don't want you to get started drinking." The doctor frowned, as if he'd forgotten something. "You haven't told me whether you're a heavy smoker."

"I smoke a pipe in the evening."

"There, again, common sense rules. Just a pipeful or two. *Absolutely, do not inhale.* Smoke only for taste. Not much is known about this killer disease. There's no medicine for it, no cure. We do know that a high, dry climate like this is helpful, though not always a cure, depending on the patient's condition when coming here. We know it can be transmitted from person to person . . . that is, we think so." He leaned back reflectively. "We have no research figures on it, but it stands to reason that tobacco smoke is an irritant and harmful to the lungs. Any smoke is. . . . Let's see, now. You've been here about six months."

"Over six months," Evan said a bit emphatically. "In fact, I haven't coughed blood for six months and twenty days."

Renshaw smiled. "So you keep track?"

"Each day."

"Before long, feeling good, you'll forget to do that."

A Mexican woman came to the outside office door, and Renshaw said: "I've kept you long enough, Evan. Just keep on as you are."

Evan thanked him, left the usual ridiculously low fee, and was at the door when a thought arrested him. "As busy as you always are, Doc, have you noticed the riders in town?"

Renshaw showed a weary smile. "I don't have to notice. The Mexicans tell me everything that goes on, here and around. What they might miss, Bear Webb picks up at the store and the Gem. Horsemen started coming in some days ago. Just a few at a time. They have a camp north of town. Sometimes they whoop it up." He released a cynical grin. "So far, no wounded have been brought in."

"What does it mean?"

"Change, no doubt, which I don't want. I love this God-given valley and river and mountains just the way they were created. Saved my life. Now saving yours, using common sense." He had to get that chiding reminder in again, always the healer.

A sharing moment passed between them, then Evan said: "You look tired, Doc. You need to take better care of yourself. Get more rest. Take some naps." Looking straight at him, smiling, he admonished: "Common sense, you know."

Renshaw's reply was to send Evan on his way with an ousting gesture.

Evan waved at Webb as he rode by. Webb shook his head in a wondering way. By now the **Land Office** sign was in place. For a moment Evan had the impulse to tie up at the saloon and visit with Cap Shaw. Most of the riders had gone by now. Doc Renshaw had echoed Evan's own feelings. But, considering it further, he rode on. Reason . . . or was it common sense? . . . told him that he was a stranger in the valley. It was not his place to get involved in local matters. He had his health to think about, first. Outsiders had the right to come in and buy land. But what if there was violence and valley people got hurt and he continued to distance himself? What then? Such inaction struck him as cold and unfeeling; it ignored the fact that he owed his life to the valley and the river and the mountains, and to people who had been unhesitatingly kind to him in many ways. He lived among friends. In turn, he ought to be a friend.

He rode out of town, troubled, sensing the beginning of change, likely great change.

Chapter Two

For days Evan stayed away from the village, resolved to maintain his detachment while embarking on a new project to occupy his time, breaking a trail northeast of the cabin. It was rather leisurely work, nothing heavy, clearing brush and smoothing out the travel with a shovel. He had no particular destination in mind other than making a way that would provide a distant view of the valley and lead to the upper reaches of the mountains. After lunch, followed by much pausing to gaze at the forested scenery and bird life, he was usually back by mid-afternoon to finish out the day reading newspapers.

Today he was outside the cabin, in his head the notion of building a little porch, when he saw a rider saddling up the trail from Rosita. The rider, an Anglo, waved, and Evan waved him on.

"I'm Dave Logan," the man said as he rode up. "I ranch on the other side of Pablo Garza's place. He suggested I drop by if I ever happened up this way. I take it you're Evan Shelby?"

"Yes. Step down and come in. Glad Pablo did. The Garzas are good friends. Been helpful to me in many ways."

Logan had a broad, friendly face with earnest brown eyes and the lean, hard appearance of a man who was accustomed to doing more than just riding the range. Evan guessed him to be in his late thirties. His soft drawl indicated Texas origin. Logan dismounted and offered his hand.

"This is not a social call," he said, smiling in a courteous way, "although that would be welcome. There'll be a meeting at the schoolhouse around two Saturday afternoon. I figured you might want to ride in, since it could concern a lot of valley folks."

"Neighborly of you to make the ride, Mister Logan. What is it?"

Logan looked down and up, seeming to gather his thoughts just how to say it. "There's a big move on to buy up valley land. I understand some El Paso bankers are behind a big Texas cow outfit. They've opened a land office in town. One lawyer-lookin' gent is doin' most of the talkin' so far."

"Have they made any offers?"

"Not yet. Just stirrin' up interest. Makin' it sound like early Christmas. On Saturday they'll get down to taw." He stopped, a troubled look creasing his face.

"Come in," Evan said. "There's warm coffee on the stove. I can't offer you anything stronger. Tie up at the corral."

"Coffee's fine. I'm obliged to you."

Logan glanced about the one-room with approval, while Evan poured the coffee. "You got the old place lookin' good. Last time I rode by here, about a year ago, part of the roof had caved in."

"I found it abandoned and moved in. Fortunately the sides were intact, and the fireplace could be built back. Mister Keeley, at the store, sent me a man. I bought the little cook stove. It heats up fast with juniper. Makes great biscuits."

Logan grinned. "Man's got to learn how to make biscuits when he's batchin'."

"I learned fast. Trial and error."

They talked a while in general about the valley before returning to the new matter. "I can see how the Mimbres would look inviting to anybody, but how would big cow outfits get cattle in here?" Evan asked.

"Trail in from the Río Grande, or from the San Simon Valley in Arizona Territory. To get started, I drove a little bunch from the Río Grande. Lost a few head on the way, but had enough left to start a small operation, then watch it grow."

"Where would they market their beef?"

"Army markets, for one. Fort Cummings and Fort Bayard. And the mining camps in the vicinity of Bayard, such as Piños Altos. I made a little cattle drive last fall down to Cummings. Army needs more beef than I can handle right now. . . . There's also talk about buildin' a railroad from El Paso to Tucson. There'd be a shippin' point south of the valley, not far from Cummings. There's no end to this. Once set up along the valley, a big outfit could take in all that great grass country on the southwest . . . plumb to the Mexican border."

"Big plans," Evan agreed. "That will take a deal of money."

"Reckon they've got it, way they blow. Get the land first. Go from there. Cattle's cheap in Texas. Bring 'em in. Meanwhile, have the politicians and promoters talk the federal government into buildin' the railroad."

"Any idea what they'll offer per acre?"

"They haven't let that out. Sorta danglin' it like a prize. A sudden few hundred dollars can seem like a fortune to a Mexican who's been poor all his life." Logan looked troubled.

"I'm sorry to hear this in more ways than one," Evan said. "The Mimbres Valley is like a hidden jewel, just now being discovered by outsiders. Question is, will they respect it and the people here?"

"The Mimbres was known about years ago. But it's a long way from Texas, then the war came along. A few Mexicans and Anglos drifted in before there was any Homestead Act . . . took what they could handle. Some that came in after that added to their hundred-sixty-acre homesteads. I came out here three years ago. Glad to get away from carpetbaggers and old family feuds in South Texas. This country will boom before long. No doubt about it. Like a keg of powder waitin' for somebody to set it off."

"What happens if some landowners with prime holdings don't choose to sell?"

"I don't like to think about that. I'm one of 'em. So is Pablo."

"I saw eight or ten riders the day I was in town. A hard-looking crew. Wonder why so many?"

Logan's frown deepened. "I asked Keeley the same question. He said for protection against Apaches."

"That makes sense as far as it goes. But after what happened in town, I wonder all the more."

Logan looked startled. "What the hell happened?"

"As I came out of the store, I saw a man about to take my Spencer from its scabbard on my horse. If I hadn't stopped him, I do believe he would have gone with it. I could tell he really coveted that carbine. I told him I'd break his arm if he removed it. Not sure I could've. He looked strong. There were riders loafing in front of the store, and, when somebody there told this man called Code to ease off, he backed off at once. Said he'd just wanted to look at it. We talked a short bit, and I rode on."

"I'll be damned! You handled it just right, in an unusual way. The man that spoke up must have been Arch Kinder. Seems to be in charge of the riders. I call him the foreman. I had a drink with 'im. Didn't learn anything. His bunch strikes me as a mixture of hardcases from all over. Some Texans." He had to grin a little. "I shore didn't ask anybody what name he went by back in the States. They all seem to be waitin' for things to pop, which I reckon they will, come Saturday."

27

Sensing still more behind this amiable man, Evan said: "I feel that likely you served in the war. Mind telling me what outfit?"

"Not a-tall. Eleventh Texas cavalry. They sent us east of the Mississippi to Joe Wheeler's corps."

"Mine was the Second Pennsylvania cavalry. Mostly in Virginia." Seeing the question in Logan's eyes, he felt the need to explain. "I came out here over six months ago for my health. I'm what is called a lunger. Everything here . . . the air, the river, the mountains . . . has combined to save my life. I can honestly say that I've never felt better. Truth is, I was desperate. I came out here to get well or die. I owe my life to this valley. The people, too."

"That's mighty good. You bet. Glad you're well."

"On the way. I'm careful about keeping dishes clean so I can't pass this on to anyone. Doc Renshaw says I'm over the hump. But give myself a year for a complete cure." Evan's face crinkled in a grin. "Meanwhile, no sprees. Never."

"Hell," Logan exclaimed with a laugh, "that'd be good advice for any man to follow. How did you know about the Mimbres?"

Evan filled him in about Fort Craig and his service prior to the war. "Our principal duty was providing escort for wagon trains along the trail in the Jornada del Muerto. We had brushes with Apaches, but never got them where we could concentrate our fire. They were clever fighters. It was chasing Chief Chato that I happened to discover the Mimbres. I thank him for that."

"We've been lucky through here. But ol' Chato's still at it. Mexicans, who seem to hear things before a white man does, tell me he's been raiding west of Fort Bayard. Some little mining camps. A man should always go armed."

"I agree to that."

As the rancher rose to leave, Evan said: "Thanks very much for coming, Mister Logan. I appreciate it. Glad to meet another Mimbres Valley man." He held out his hand.

"It's Dave." Logan's work-hardened grip was quick and true.

"I'll be at the meeting," Evan said.

As Logan rode off, it occurred to Evan that there went a good man, and not one senseless damn' word between them about the war. In his musing, he sensed that he was going to stay here past this year. Likely for the rest of his days. He relished the very happy thought. How fortunate could a man be!

Saturday afternoon Evan left the Spencer in the cabin, stuck the .44 revolver in his waistband, and rode for Rosita.

He could feel the freshened pulse of the village before he reached it, the meshing of voices and the creaks and chain rattles of wagons and teams and, to his surprise, catchy banjo music.

Wagons and buggies crowded the street and overflowed under the cottonwoods toward the river. Saddle horses lined the hitching racks. There was a constant going in and out at Keeley's store and the Gem. Over all, the hum of voices.

Several people stood in close conversation on the hotel's verandah. Among them a shapely young woman in a light-blue suit of a style he hadn't seen since Philadelphia and New York. She stood quite slim and self-composed, and her well-molded face under the small flowered hat suddenly struck him as features a man would remember, her appealing image like a print on his mind as he rode on. Others besides Evan were staring at her unusual presence here. He supposed that she, a stranger, might have something to do with the meeting.

The banjo music, emanating from the steps of the schoolhouse, had drawn a considerable crowd for Rosita. A genial black man tapped his foot in time to his lively music, and his smile knew no strangers. Looking back on his own youth, Evan appreciated the music all the more. People were hungry for entertainment, even out here in their splendid isolation. The scene would be complete, he thought, with a silver-tongued barker extolling the many restorative powers of some wonderful elixir, and, at the right moment, a shill eagerly stepping up to buy the first bottle. Only a dollar, folks.

Evan tied up near the doctor's office and strolled back to the schoolhouse, his interest growing as he watched the crowd. Anglos and Mexicans about evenly numbered. Across the way Pablo and Josefa Garza. Dave Logan was headed this way, no doubt from the Gem. After some minutes, a portly man dressed in a brown business suit left the verandah of the hotel and passed through the crowd, smiling all the way. He nodded to the black man, who ceased playing, stood, and bowed to the applauding crowd and stepped down.

"Friends," the portly man said, raising his voice, "you are cordially invited now to come inside for the meeting." So saying, he opened the door and stood aside like a respectful doorman.

The crowd followed, somewhat hesitantly at first, then began a general movement inside. Waiting until most had entered, Evan found standing room at the rear. Although only a one-room school, it was long and wide and adequate as the crowd, many self-consciously, filled the students' short benches and sat at their desks.

Shortly, a stir at the door drew Evan's attention to the young woman of the verandah entering on the arm of an older man. A broad, muscular individual, a chesty man wearing a wide-brimmed hat. He stood above those around him and seemed packed with energy. He had an aggressive cast to his square-jawed face and bold gray eyes with thick brows. He flashed even, white teeth as he said something and smiled down at the woman and removed his hat. He was, Evan saw, being very correct, very attentive, and also quite possessive in a manner that he wanted those around him to notice.

A proud, forceful man, Evan thought. *Arch Kinder, the foreman?*

As the crowd settled and voices stilled to whispers, the portly man in the brown suit went to the front and, ever smiling, nodding about, began speaking in a pleasant voice that carried clearly over the room.

"Friends of the Mimbres Valley, I am R.C. Conklin, special representative of the famed Empire Cattle Company of San Antonio, Texas." His double chin wobbled as he spoke. "I've met some of you folks. Those I haven't, I'm looking forward to meeting and knowing. Empire thanks all of you for journeying here today."

A smooth talker, Evan observed. A salesman. Convincing, with some bullshit thrown in.

"But before we get started," Conklin said, "I should like to make a special introduction." Looking toward the entrance of the room, he said: "Miss Lucinda, will you come forward, please?"

Smiling, the comely young woman of the verandah began making her way through the crowd. As she neared Conklin, he made a sweeping gesture of introduction and boomed: "It is my distinct honor and pleasure to present to you folks, Miss Lucinda Holloway, owner of Empire Cattle, and daughter of the late Rip Holloway . . . famous in Texas as a trail-blazing cowman and Indian fighter."

He commenced applauding, and the crowd, with obvious interest, courteously joined in at once.

Flushing prettily, she thanked him and turned to the crowd. "I am, indeed, happy to be here and hope that we of

31

Empire can share some of this beautiful valley with you and always remain your good neighbors."

Her sincere, genteel voice, Evan thought, went with what a man saw. Warm, wide eyes, which he decided at this distance were blue, and a sweet smile. Dark-brown hair under that little hat. He liked the way she held her head: composed, with an air of open friendliness.

In the next instant, she was speaking frankly. "Just because I'm dressed up a little today, don't think I go around like this all the time. I grew up on a ranch. My father always insisted I dress up before I went to town. Take a bath first, he ordered, and sometimes I had to take it in a creek. Any water's good in Southwest Texas." A man's hearty laugh set off a ripple of laughter. "He even sent me off to a finishing school in Saint Louis, but I survived it. It didn't finish me." Everybody seemed to be smiling. "There are other things to talk about today. But I want to leave you with what my father used to say and what he went by. He said . . . 'To be a good neighbor, sometimes you have to go to hell for somebody. Sometimes you even have to go to hell with 'em.' Well, Empire wants to be that kind of neighbor."

Evan applauded with the rest. *Well said. Can't beat that. But would she be the one handling negotiations? Probably not.*

She smiled graciously every step of the way back. Almost any man, Evan thought, would do his damnedest to please her. Or was he overly impressed because he had long been denied the company of such a sweet and engaging young woman? On second thought, he decided not.

Evan could feel an air of expectancy after Conklin thanked Miss Holloway, smiled expansively, cleared his throat, and said: "I know you're all wondering what Empire will pay for grazing land. Well, first of all, Empire will be fair, even generous."

"How much are you offerin'?" a white man asked.

"Depends on the location. For holdings along the river, Empire will pay more."

"Ever'body's got access to the river. Nobody gets fenced off from water. We're all good neighbors." He gave a crooked smile. "At least, most folks are." The man had a thin, leathery face and was bent, which to Evan told of hard times.

"That's what I want to hear," Conklin said, ever agreeable.

Another man asked: "Why does Empire want to come into New Mexico? Ain't there plenty of range left in Texas?"

Conklin showed the quick smile of a man who had an answer for any question. He said: "It's expansion. Everything moves westward in this country. And there's only one Mimbres Valley. Water, grass, wood, and unbeatable climate."

Evan turned that over in his mind, thinking what Dave Logan had told him about range to the southwest for the taking and, in the future, the potential of a railroad and a shipping point.

"Let's cut this a little finer," the leathery-faced man said. "Get down to how much an acre Empire will offer."

"Again, as I said back there, much depends on the location. For a good sweep of land along the river, Empire will pay as much as two dollars an acre. A dollar for upland ranches. Maybe more."

Evan knew that was too low and heard a collective murmur of disappointment. Men exchanged looks. For further affirmation, he saw Logan's look of disgust.

"Now that's hard money on the barrelhead," Conklin followed up, "and Empire might pay more after our representatives ride over the land."

As low as the initial figures were, Evan saw some heads

turned in consideration, and he remembered Logan's words that a few hundred dollars might seem like a fortune to a man who'd been poor all his life.

Another man asked: "Is Empire gonna have to have its range all in one big block?"

"That would be ideal," Conklin replied, "but not absolutely necessary. Empire could operate with a range of big pastures. If the grass got grazed down in one pasture, stock could be moved to another pasture that hadn't been grazed hard . . . say, in a dry spell."

A contemplative silence followed, broken only when Conklin said: "You folks who want to talk money today can go across the street to the land office, and we'll sit down and work things out. Where your place is located? How many acres? When we send riders out to look it over? Of course, we've already talked to some of you and know the details. . . . When we agree on a deal, you'll get your money right away at Mister Keeley's. We're handling our banking through him for your convenience. You won't have to go to Las Cruces or El Paso to get your money. Just go to the store. Like I said, it's money on the barrelhead."

As the silence hung on, the conflict of uncertainty and quick money, Evan tensed, expecting Logan to offer words of caution. But he did not. Why didn't somebody speak up? Why didn't somebody tell Conklin that Empire would have to raise the ante? Two dollars an acre for grazing land along the river! A dollar for upland ranches? Conklin was waving a pittance of ready money in front of these hard-working people, making it look so easy.

Still, no man spoke up.

Something had to give in, but didn't.

It flashed through Evan's mind that Mimbres people, particularly the Mexicans, were not used to speaking in public or questioning a person of authority. As the silence persisted and Conklin started to close the meeting, Evan discovered himself raising his right hand and speaking in a distinct voice: "Mister Conklin, may I say something, please?"

He was suddenly aware of being the center of attention. He caught Conklin's frown, an obliging smile quickly in place, and Conklin said: "Yes, indeed. Do you have a question?"

"Not a question, no, sir. Just a few words of caution to all of you people of the valley. Think before you rush to sell your land at these low prices. Where would you go if you sold out? Some of you came here years ago from Chihuahua to escape the oppression of wealthy *hacendados*. Would you go back there? To a place you left so you could be free and have land of your own and a home? Would . . . ?"

"Sir, sir," Conklin broke in. "Are you a landowner?"

"I am not. But I hope to have a homestead before long. The Mimbres is a wonderful place to live. So are its people. I've been here some six months."

"Would you identify yourself, sir?"

"Glad to. I am Evan Shelby, late a captain in the Union cavalry, Second Pennsylvania, during the war. Before the war, I served at Fort Craig, on the Río Grande."

That quickened more keen looks.

"Of course, you have the right to speak at this public meeting. But . . . if I may say so . . . you are virtually disrupting it with your line of talk, Mister . . . ah . . . Captain Shelby."

"On the other hand, sir, somebody should interrupt before people get hurt and there's a rush for quick money. In all due respect, Mister Conklin, I dare say the prices you've quoted are far below actual value."

Now he'd done it, he realized, stuck his neck out. Got

himself—an outsider—a Yankee to boot—involved against his better judgment in local matters not of his affair. But he lived here. He felt an obligation.

These bits flew through his head as Conklin, fast on his feet, shot back in a tone on the verge of belittlement. "Who are you, Captain Shelby, to say prices are too low? Are you a qualified assessor, sir? An authority on land prices in New Mexico Territory?"

"I am not an authority. But reasoning tells me they're too low."

Conklin uttered a low laugh. "There has to be a basis or comparison for you to take that stand, sir. I am going by land prices along the Río Grande."

"Except this is better land. Better water. Better climate. My other basis is common sense, and what I've learned living here. I believe Mimbres land is worth more than quoted. Furthermore, landowners should stop and think before they take the leap at these prices. It's their decision. They need to rock back and forth, horse trade a little."

He was set for Conklin to ask him what prices were fair, and he was going to say four or five dollars an acre along the river. But, in a moment, he sensed that Conklin was too cagey to get any higher figures out before these people.

Instead, Conklin asked, in an easing voice, "Sir, if I offered to sell you a good-looking saddler, say, for fifty dollars, would you buy the horse immediately?"

"I might be tempted at that price," Evan replied with a grin, "but first I'd look at his teeth."

Spontaneous laughter broke, running from person to person, and Conklin quickly followed with: "By the same token, Captain Shelby, Empire wants the good people of the Mimbres Valley to look at its offers in the teeth. And when they do, they'll find them fair and sound. . . . Now, folks,

Empire thanks you for coming here today, and those of you who wish to talk further, we'll look for you at the land office. Thank you very much."

Conklin had held his temper in check, but his face was beet-red and he could not hide his displeasure. He threw Evan a cutting look, and by that Evan knew that the Empire man had lost the moment just when he had the crowd going his way. Quickly, the smile pasted back on, he slipped away through the crowd.

Valley people were looking at Evan in a friendly manner. Some nodded. On the other hand, the imposing-looking man Evan had taken for Arch Kinder sent him a blunt message across the room that said: *Mind your own business.* In an obvious proprietary manner, he escorted Miss Holloway outside.

Logan was waiting for Evan near the entrance. Drawing him aside, he slapped Evan on the back, saying: "Thanks for standing up. Somebody needed to."

"Why didn't you? I kept looking for you."

Logan looked down. "Truth is, I ain't much on public speakin'. Mostly to cows. I kept hopin' somebody would."

"At least, it got said. Maybe folks will think before they leap. Was that Arch Kinder with Miss Holloway?"

"Yeah."

"I gather that he didn't like what I said, judging by the look he gave me. Like I was interfering."

"He would, bein' the ramrod. Stands to be the big stud, if Empire takes over the valley. Shore kept close to that purty Miss Holloway, didn't he? Like he was standin' guard. . . . Let's have a drink."

"I'd like something. Guess I can have a beer."

"You can have sarsaparilla if you want it, an' nobody'd better laugh."

"If they did, I might laugh with 'em. Don't recall I've ever had any."

The crowd was slow breaking up, neighbors visiting and discussing the meeting. Two men came over and shook Evan's hand, to his vast discomfort. Across the way an elderly Mexican man was heading for the land office.

"Goin' for that barrelhead money," Logan commented dryly. "Old man Moreno. Lives up the valley. Gettin' old. Might sell. Go live with a daughter in Las Cruces. Couldn't blame him."

The Garzas joined them. Pablo looked serious. "*Señor* Evan, what you said was good. People should think a long time before they sell. Where would they go? What would happen to them?"

"Reckon Empire has been out your way?" Logan ventured.

Pablo nodded.

"Mind sayin' what they offered you?"

"Two dollars an acre."

"And you've got a nice place along the river."

"I no sell for that."

"Good. We don't want you to leave. Want to keep you folks here."

As others drifted over to visit with the Garzas, Evan went on with Logan, who muttered: "Offer a man enough money and he'll sell anything."

"Five dollars an acre?" Evan asked.

"No. But Empire had better not offer me eight."

"Don't worry. They won't."

The Gem was crowded and loud, and Evan noticed Empire riders grouped at the far end of the bar. Among them was the man called Code, whom Evan had glimpsed at the schoolhouse.

"What'll you have?" Logan asked him.

"I'll stick with beer."

As Cap Shaw set their drinks down, Evan asked him in a light way: "Not that I want any, Cap, but do you happen to have any sarsaparilla?"

Shaw brushed at his proud handlebar mustache and grinned. "Don't carry it. Might start a fight. Somebody's manhood might be questioned if he got caught sippin' it. I've seen a man or two shot over the stuff. An' there's the old gunfighter sayin' back in the Lone Star State . . . 'I'll take no sass but sarsaparilla.' "

"Pretty good." Evan smiled. "I hadn't heard that. If I ever go back there, I'll keep that in mind."

They sipped a while. Then Logan, in a low voice, said: "Back in Texas in the early days Empire was known as a hard outfit. Ran roughshod over some folks. Took over water holes. Empire cattle seemed to increase at an amazin' rate. One joke was their cows would have two calves. It was common talk they kept their brandin' iron smooth and swung a wide loop. Not that Empire was the only outfit doin' it. Yep, they say ol' Rip Holloway got rich. . . . But folks gave him credit for two things . . . he was generous when a neighbor family hit hard times or ran into hard luck. Say, there was a death in the family. He'd give the shirt off his back. Nobody went hungry. He'd been hungry himself. He was also a fightin' son-of-a-bitch . . . cleared out the Comanches mighty good and thinned out the bandits along the border."

"What about Arch Kinder?"

"I think he goes way back with Empire. Was Rip's *segundo*."

"What's that, Dave?"

"Assistant trail boss or second in command. Foreman."

The saloon was constantly stirring, and somehow Evan

was not surprised when the rider he knew as Code eased over his way. Pushing his glance at Evan, he had that glittery look of the day of the carbine and he was armed as before, wearing his gun low, as if it were part of him.

"Say, Yank, you kinda put a kink in the meetin'. Just when folks got in the mood to make some deals."

"There's still plenty of time to make deals. But people need to think before they sell their farms and ranches. That was all I had in mind. Not to rush."

"Nobody else spoke up but you."

Around them the murmur of voices suddenly shut off. Stillness lay over the room.

Logan broke in: "Other people wanted to, but held back. I was one of 'em. Might say Captain Shelby spoke for more than one of us. Did us a favor. Valley folks ain't used to makin' a breeze in public places."

"Sounds like you're making excuses for a greenhorn."

"He's trying to explain it to you," Evan put in. "If you have anything to say to me, say it." He was rather surprised at himself, at the sharp jolt of anger he felt, and he knew it sharpened his voice. He also became suddenly sensitive to the feel of the .44 at his waistband.

Code threw a challenging look at him. "Shore, I got somethin' to say to you." Deliberately he seemed to delay to give emphasis on what he was about to say.

"Say it!" Evan snapped.

"You're not, a true valley man. Understand you're a stranger here. So stay outta this."

"That sounds like a threat."

"Call it what you like."

Then, for further effect, Code slowly sauntered toward the other end of the bar and the riders.

Voices picked up again.

Evan just shook his head, caught in the grip of unreality. It was outright ridiculous for a man to threaten and take that stand.

"I'll be damned," Logan muttered. "Haven't heard that kind of gun talk since I left Texas, and one damn' good reason why I left."

"Let's finish our drinks," Evan said calmly.

"I don't like this. You'll have to keep a sharp eye, Evan."

"I just had a sad thought, Dave. Can you imagine a man, in fear of his life, forced to sell out choice grazing land for a few dollars? Not an outright threat, mind you. Just a veiled hint of what might happen, all the same."

They finished drinking, and, as they started to leave, Evan saw that Code and his bunch were watching him. Something stirred in Evan, and he turned and faced Code and said: "I hadn't intended to get into this at all. But, hereon, I'll help valley people any way I can to get a fair price for their land. You can take that any way you like."

He waited for Code to make a move. Code didn't. A slack-jawed surprise flickered across his face.

He figured he had me bluffed, Evan thought.

Walking out, behind him a deep well of silence, Evan knew that he had been forced to take the one step he'd tried to avoid. He'd merely wanted to help valley people. But now he had committed himself in public, and there could be no turning back. The realization left him suddenly depressed.

Chapter Three

Lucinda Holloway stood by the window in her room at the Mimbres Hotel, watching with interest the flow of people along the dusty street after the meeting. Much visiting by families. She liked neighborliness. Rosita was such a pretty name for the village. In time it would become a prosperous town with Empire behind its growth. It needed a little store or shop for women—the finer things. Valley people, a mixture of Anglos and Mexicans, small ranchers and farmers, struck her as reserved yet friendly with strangers. She could still see their open faces as she talked to them. She smiled at the recollection of their awe at a woman, particularly a young woman, speaking in public, that alone had impressed them.

She noticed the tall man who had spoken up at the last moment, now entering the Gem Saloon with a rancher. Shelby, she recalled. Evan Shelby. A Yankee. Well, all Yankees couldn't be the stiff-necked New Englanders or conniving carpetbaggers of her limited knowledge of the breed. Shelby had seemed out of place here until he'd explained serving on the Río Grande before the war. She judged him a fair-minded man, although not well informed on current land prices, based on his exchange with R.C. Conklin, who was actually furious at having his spiel interrupted. Were Empire's offers really too low? She recalled what her crusty father had said: the price of anything from stock to land was what the other person would agree to.

She turned at a rap at the door and felt a sharp annoyance as Arch Kinder entered immediately with a look of anticipation. He came straight to her and would have kissed her on the lips had she not drawn away, saying: "Arch, you should not enter a room without being invited in. It's rude and assuming."

He refused to show hurt feelings. He smiled his great smile at her and said: "Aw, Cindy, you know how I feel about you."

She shook her head at him. "It's common courtesy not to barge in like that, whether a man or woman is in the room." She had never allowed him to kiss her on the lips. In recent months since her father's death, he had become more aggressively possessive. Sometimes she felt an actual physical fear of Arch Kinder, Empire's *segundo* for almost as long as she could remember. Yet he was a good cowman, and she needed him to run Empire's vast holdings of land and stock.

"You're right, shore," he admitted. "I didn't mean to be rude. You were still big in my mind after the meetin'. All I could think of was how you stood up there and talked. It was plumb good, and I was mighty proud of you."

"Thank you." She wanted to be courteous, yet not lead him on. There were times when Arch Kinder could approach humility, although never completely, and she felt a twinge of regret for her curtness.

"You see, Cindy, you were just a little tyke when I started ridin' for your father. I was a wild kid, nineteen years old. Had lost my folks on the Brazos . . . Comanches. Your father took me in . . . settled me down. Don't think I ever told you all o' this. If he hadn't, I would've hit the Owlhoot Trail . . . been an outlaw on the dodge. He saved my hide. Made a man of me. I owe him an' his memory everything. He was like a father to me."

She caught the quickening intensity in his eyes as he moved toward her to take her in his arms. She did not step back; instead, she gave him her left cheek, and, as he started to reach for her, she pushed him back. He stopped, but his performance of near humility had vanished in a flash.

"I thought we were going to discuss signing up land-owners," she reminded him. "I have affection for you, Arch. I appreciate what you did for Father and what you are doing now to carry out his dream of a ranch in the Mimbres Valley. But I'm not ready to consider marriage to any man."

"You will with me in time," he declared, smiling again. "The Mimbres is one of the best herding grounds in New Mexico. Together we can make it the biggest spread in the territory."

"Sometimes I wonder that having the biggest wasn't what Father really had in mind."

"Why not?"

"One evening not long before he died"—she avoided saying *killed*—"he kept talking about peace of mind. As a young man, he had traveled through the lower Mimbres with cowmen bound for Arizona, hoping to start up a ranch out there. Prospects didn't work out, and they went back to Texas by a lower trail. . . . He never saw the Mimbres again, but he never forgot the valley and its good water, grass up to his latigo straps, the lazy cottonwoods and the cool mountains in the distance. It was always there, in the back of his mind. Texas took over. No end to the struggle of building a ranch, fighting Comanche raiders, Anglo thieves, and gangs of *bandidos* from across the Río Grande. I know he still longed for the peace he never had when he died. It was his last hope that we establish Empire out here, even sell out in Texas, if necessary, and if we think we can make a go of it."

"No *ifs* about it. We're gonna make it . . . make it big."

"You sound very confident."

"Rip taught me that."

"How?"

"Just do it. A little pressure here and there can swing a deal."

"Pressure? Just how do you mean?"

"Easy. Just show a man it would be to his advantage if he agrees to our offer."

She regarded him for a long moment. "I believe you are talking about forcing people to sell?"

Arch Kinder was not a man who revealed himself easily, and he did not now. He laughed it off. "Now, Cindy, I'm not talkin' about pokin' a gun in a man's ribs."

"Then what are you saying?"

"Wave money in a man's face and point out it's his only offer. That no other outfit is comin' in here with money on the barrelhead."

"That is true," she agreed. "The valley is remote."

"Take it or leave it. A fistful o' ready money will look mighty good to most folks."

"How do you plan to go about this?"

"Well, tomorrow Conklin and me and the boys will start makin' the rounds. After talkin' to Keeley at the store, we aim to work the lower Mimbres first. Some nice holdings down there."

"You say *the boys*. How many have come in?"

"Ten, countin' Code Sloan."

A curious note entered her voice. "Who are these so-called *boys?*"

He shrugged it off with a grin. "Not a Sunday school-teacher in the bunch, you can bet on that. They've been cowpunchers and other things. Some have been in trouble with the law. But not a man is now wanted by the rangers or is on the dodge from elsewhere. They're men I can depend on. They won't back off from a fight, but they won't start one unless I say so. . . . I mentioned Code Sloan. He's the big augur of the bunch."

"But why so many riders?"

"Remember, this is also Apache country."

"I haven't forgotten. What are you paying these men with my money? Not cowpuncher's wages, I'm sure."

He didn't bat an eye as he replied, "A hundred dollars a month and grub. An' worth ever' cent, if we need 'em. Right now they're camped near town."

"A hundred dollars a month?" she questioned. "That's far more than Father ever paid riders."

"This is New Mexico. These are dangerous times. Besides, we need to make a show . . . look like a big outfit."

"We're big enough," she said. Although that was considerable money to be going out each month, she protested no further. Arch had acted on her general authority, which she realized her father would have given him as *segundo*. Not only had Rip Holloway left Empire on solid financial footing, but she also had the backing of bankers in El Paso, old friends of the family whom she knew personally.

"Are you planning on bringing in more men?" she asked.

"Not yet."

"Why would you need more men?"

"You never know what might come up."

She didn't like the trend of their conversation, the vagueness. "Ten riders should be more than enough, unless you're thinking of a range war." She was exaggerating, and he knew it.

"I try to go by what Rip Holloway taught me." When she did not take that up, he said: "In any new situation, don't go in half-cocked. Be ready if trouble breaks so you can get out."

"I can't imagine a situation with valley landowners where you might have to shoot your way out."

"Anything might happen anywhere, Cindy. You know that."

"In Texas, at least," she amended. "And down along the border. Not among these people."

They were getting nowhere, and, having no desire to continue it further, she added nothing. Sensing it was time to go, he smiled, and, when he made again to embrace and kiss her, she lifted her hands in a warding-off gesture. "Arch, I don't want to have to push you away every time I see you in private. I'm tired of it."

"Then let me love you."

"No, Arch. No. Please . . . you just make it difficult. Let us remain good friends as we've always been."

He stood back, virile and straight, his strong-jawed face hardening. "Someday," he said, "you'll understand and be damned glad you've got Arch Kinder to lean on," and strode out.

She was rigid. There had been no mock humility in what he'd just said. It was more like a threat or prophecy. Regret welled up as she thought of the past and all that Arch Kinder had meant to her father and to Empire, yet with that stirred the fear she was beginning to feel every time she was alone with him—that something was about to happen.

And the ten riders he'd hired. All hardcases, he'd admitted. Why hadn't he brought in somebody who rode for the brand? A trusted man like Hap McCoy, who was getting on in years but could still mount up every day? Hap had taught her to ride and how to take care of a horse, later, how to handle a rifle. Near her father's age, Hap went back before Arch Kinder. She missed Hap. She wanted him out here. She felt she needed him.

Shaken, she sat down to compose herself, feeling the onset of loneliness, thinking of her father. At the ranch she would have saddled a horse and gone riding, mindful as always of Comanches and bands of thieving riders swooping in from the border, a rifle sheathed on her saddle. Here she was tied down. If this land business dragged on and on, she intended to get out more. In moments like this, her mind often turned to her dear, long-ago mother, only a dim face in the tintype, loving the large, expressive eyes in the fine features with the hint of a hidden smile and the sweetness there. Lucinda knew that her own features with high cheek bones stood out more. Yet it had pleased her when her father had said she had a strong resemblance to her mother.

Rip Holloway had never talked at any length about the young wife who had died of pneumonia, leaving him with a three-year-old daughter to raise on a frontier ranch, fighting for existence in Southwest Texas. Sometimes he had almost choked up when Lucinda had asked particulars about her mother. The tone of her voice? How she dressed? Her likes and dislikes? Other times he would look down or away with a few words. It had become so painful for him that in recent years she had mentioned her mother, whose name was Mary Elizabeth, only in passing. He had left Lucinda in charge of gentle, doting Mexican women, while he threw himself into building the ranch and fighting invaders. Hearing her speaking Spanish, he would smile and say she was half Mexican. He had been, indeed, a loving father, constantly holding and playing with her and carrying her about the house and outside to the corrals to see the horses, or calves and goats and, when she had begged, taking her in the saddle with him for a ride. When he had to be gone, she would watch for hours by a living room window for a familiar head-nodding horse and lean rider to take shape out of the prairie vastness.

Still in need, she now went downstairs and found Hannah Young busy instructing a young Mexican girl about setting the four small tables in the little dining room, which shared space with the cramped hotel lobby and desk and three raw-hide-covered chairs.

Mrs. Young noticed her at once and came to her and greeted her in a most pleasant voice: "We're getting ready early for supper. What can this old ranch woman do for you?" And when Lucinda hesitated—"You look tired. Sit down. I'll get you some coffee . . . real cowboy coffee . . . which is the only kind we serve here."

Lucinda smiled at that. "Oh, thank you, but never mind now. I want to ask you something, Missus Young. Since I may be in Rosita for a while, I was thinking of renting a small adobe house Mister Keeley has offered. But, frankly, I'd rather stay here and make it my headquarters . . . if that wouldn't cause too much coming in and out?"

"Child, don't you dare rent that old, rundown 'dobe. Anything to make a buck . . . that's Keeley, though he is our main-stay. You stay here with Hannah Young. You'll have complete privacy, with no rough stuff, and a clean place to live as long as you wish to stay."

"I would like that. Thank you very much."

"And good ranch meals. Biscuits and cornbread. Chiles to go with the beans and bacon and plenty of vegetables and fruit pies and preserves. We raise a lot of fruit along the valley." She put a forefinger to her lips. "As for the rate, would fifty cents a day for the room and fifty cents for all the meals be all right?"

"For me, yes. But not for you. You'll be broke at those rates."

Hannah Young cocked a blue eye at her. "You don't know what I charge these men. They eat like wolves. Too, you will be a special guest. Let's go into my room to visit." She invited Lucinda into a tidy room off the lobby that she used for a bedroom and office. And when they were seated, she folded her

49

plump hands across her lap and said: "I don't like for help to hear all my business, not that there's much to tell. . . . When my husband Matt passed away eight years ago, I leased out the ranch and moved to town so I'd have somebody to talk to. Built this little place . . . keeps me busy. I don't allow drunks or any whoop-'em goin's on. You'll have all the quiet you need to conduct your business."

"Thank you again, Missus Young. You are very kind and generous."

"Call me Hannah."

"The man who came in a while ago is Mister Arch Kinder, my ranch foreman. He'll be in and out. So will Mister R.C. Conklin, our main attorney. They'll both be talking to land-owners. So will I."

"Mister Kinder struck me as a genuine cowman when he came in and asked for you. Very courteous."

"He rode many years for my father."

Hannah regarded her with the intuitive eyes of a much older woman. "You don't seem excited about starting a new ranch."

"I am. But I don't want anyone hurt, or anyone to feel they have to sell."

"Of course not. Don't worry. To me, as a valley rancher for years, it's the newness and excitement of it . . . of a big outfit coming in and offering to buy range. Makes people think . . . whether to stay or move on. Life isn't easy, even when you live in extra good ranch country like on the Mimbres. You still have to work and work very hard. Don't worry."

Lucinda smiled back at her. "It's good to talk to you, Hannah. You see, what I'm doing is following through on my late father's dream. He had always longed for a ranch on the peaceful Mimbres. That's why I'm here. I promised him I would before he died."

"You're a mighty loyal daughter. Was it a family matter? You haven't mentioned your mother." Sensing, Hannah suddenly checked herself. "I hope I'm not bringing up sad memories."

"Thank you for asking. My mother passed away when I was three. Father raised me with the kind help of Mexican women."

"I'm sorry to hear about that. Very sorry."

"Thank you."

"I hope they spoiled you just a little bit?"

Lucinda laughed. "They did. More than that sometimes . . . until Father got after them. When he rode off, they went right back to doting on me."

"That's good. Don't feel apologetic. Every child who is loved is spoiled a little at times. A child needs that. It proves there is love."

"You make me feel much better," Lucinda said, openly pleased, not until now realizing the low depths of her spirit after her clash with Arch Kinder.

They both fell silent, Hannah, with a calling back in her eyes, thoughtfully observing Lucinda, then saying: "My Margaret would be about your age."

"Would?" Lucinda echoed, startled.

"We had a very hard winter. Unusual for the valley. She got sick. Coughing and fever. Doc Renshaw did all he could, that good man. Nothing seemed to help . . . so we lost her. She was only four."

"Oh, no. I'm so sorry, Hannah." Impulsively Lucinda rose and hugged Hannah. They held each other.

"I didn't mean to let myself go," Hannah said, after a moment, dabbing at her eyes. "But looking at you seemed to bring everything back. I kept seeing my Margaret grown up in you. I still do . . . as she would be now. . . . A pretty young lady

51

like you." She suddenly brightened. "I'm so glad you're here, Miss Holloway. God bless you. You make me happy again." Her eyes were glistening.

"I'm happy, too, thanks to you. And we are friends."

Chapter Four

Next morning she watched from her window as Arch Kinder and R.C. Conklin, accompanied by the ten riders, rode south out of town at a fast trot. A disturbing impression began to build as she followed them out of sight. That many men riding up to a lonely ranch or farm house could look more like a threat than a friendly call about buying grazing land.

She shook her head. She was thinking too much, troubled by the direction of her relationship with her foreman, or *segundo,* in Texas trail talk. Arch Kinder was a strong-willed man, not one to pull back from what he wanted—she knew that, having seen it demonstrated during her growing up. Rip Holloway was the only person he had deferred to, simply because his future lay with Empire.

After supper, she had visited late into the evening with Hannah Young. Lucinda knew that she had found a true and needed friend in the valley; in return, she hoped that she had helped dispel just a little of that sad emptiness in Hannah's life.

Lucinda said that she had brought her sidesaddle and rifle. Did Hannah think the liveryman would have a spare mount she might hire? If he didn't, Hannah said, she would have one brought in from her own ranch, at the same time cautioning Lucinda against long, solitary rides into the mountains.

They had parted with hugs, Lucinda going to her room with the first real uplift she had felt since her father's sudden passing, hardly more than three months ago, which still seemed like yesterday. He had died as he had lived, struggling, fighting, found by a ranch *vaquero* on the prairie, his loyal old cow horse Hondo beside him, reins down. Not far away, in front of him, lay two dead *bandidos*.

After a ranch-style breakfast, Lucinda pushing away Hannah's insistent extra helpings, she wrote a letter to Hap McCoy:

Dear Hap:
    I need you out here. Go to the bank and show them this letter and draw money on the ranch account. Don't short yourself. Remember, you have to eat and sleep. Have a drink on me. From El Paso you will change stages at Mesilla for Rosita. Bring your saddle and guns.
    Please come. I need you.

Love,
Lucinda

Hap would come. She knew he would. He rode for the brand, her dearest person, now that her father was gone. She was moving by instinct at this point. Since yesterday the realization had kept growing that she needed a trusted friend with her.

It was also time to do something here. Ten minutes later she was at the Acme Livery. She introduced herself to Silas Brown and held out her hand. Somewhat taken aback, he gallantly swept off his hat and said: "What can I do for you, Miss Holloway?"

"I'd like to rent a saddle horse."

He reflected a moment. "Your people took my two youngest horses this morning. I have an eight-year-old dark bay you might like."

"Let me see him, please."

When he led forth the bay, she smilingly inquired: "Does he have any bad habits?"

Brown, a tall, rawboned man with genial eyes in a lean face, smiled back at her. "Like me, ol' Barney's too old to pick up any new ones. He's a ranch horse. Was broke right. Likes to get down the road. Must have some saddle horse blood in his family tree, because he has a nice runnin' walk. He's all right. I believe you'll like Barney."

"I like his head and the way he stands. I shall take Barney. What is the rate, Mister Brown?"

"Two dollars a day." He looked apologetic. "Sorry, I don't have a sidesaddle."

"I have my own."

He nodded approvingly. "A ranch girl *would* come prepared. Can I bring your saddle over? Be glad to."

"I'll do that. Thank you."

Shortly, dressed in bench-made boots, riding skirt and blouse and a wide-brimmed hat with a low crown, she brought the saddle and rifle in its sheath, and a canteen, the last at Hannah Young's insistence. Her spurs made a lively jingle.

Bear Webb was busy grooming the bay. He kept his face half hidden as he spoke. "Hope I didn't frighten you, ma'am. I got tangled up with a grizzly bear years ago, and I shock people when they first see me. Why they call me Bear Webb. My first name is Jim."

"I'm sorry, Jim." She offered a gracious hand. Her grip was firm. "You don't shock me at all. Pleased to meet you. Nice of you to groom my horse."

As he took her hand with great solicitous care, he removed his sweat-stained, wretched old hat and exposed the wavy black hair of a man who once would have been considered

55

handsome. "It's mighty nice to see you, Miss Holloway. I was down the street when you came in. Now I'll saddle Barney for you."

He laid on a bright saddle blanket, cinched up, made sure of rifle and sheath and canteen and handed her the reins. She thanked him with another smile that went all through him. He would have given her a hand up, but she mounted easily on her own and reined away.

"There," said Brown, coming from his office, "goes a mighty well brought-up young lady. She couldn't have been any nicer. I was about ready to give her the place if she'd wanted it."

Webb chuckled. "Makes a man realize there's more to life than trappin' in the mountains an' livin' like a lone wolf." Worriedly he added: "I hope she's careful about ridin' around. She didn't say where she's goin'."

"She's independent, raised that way. Evan brought her own saddle and rifle. Imagine! But, hell, Bear, they're still fightin' Comanches in Texas."

"We ain't exactly on speakin' terms here with Apaches. With summer comin' on, man needs to ride extra careful."

"As plumb nice as Miss Holloway is, I can't say much for the outfit Empire's brought in. When Kinder and Conklin rented horses, you'd 'a' thought they's doin' me a big favor, the way they acted. High and mighty. Like they might own me someday. Like hell they will! Burned me up. What do you hear around and at the Gem?"

"Cap Shaw, you remember, rode for outfits in Texas 'fore he came out here. He says this *hombre* Code Sloan served time in prison for a killin'. Tough bunch. They keep to themselves at the Gem. Arch Kinder joins 'em now and then."

"You know, Bear, with Kinder throwin' his weight around and Empire pushin' for range, I think we're gonna see a heap o' things change in this valley before it's peaceful again."

" 'Fraid so, Silas. Just hope Miss Holloway comes out all right."

"Bear, I believe we're both smitten!"

She felt a growing pleasure, absent too long, as she loosened reins and the bay horse stretched out into an easy running walk, taking to the sandy footing along the winding river road. An old saying rose to her mind when riding a smooth-gaited horse: "You could drink a cup of coffee on him and never spill a drop." She leaned and spoke softly into the fox ears—"Barney, you're a real sweetheart."—and patted his neck. He also reined nicely.

The lofty cottonwoods and the sun on the broad stretches of pasture and patches of farm land passed pleasantly before her eyes. The breeze playing on her face was gentle and cool. She met no one. She rode relaxed. Twice she heard distant voices along the river.

After an hour or more she decided that she had gone far enough in a land she didn't know. She let her good horse drink at the inviting river, rested him a while, just killing time, and started back, Barney still the eager traveler as before. She might offer to buy him if everything went well with Mister Brown, who seemed like a very nice man, and Bear, too.

As she rode along, Arch Kinder troubled her. If he didn't stick to his duties and persisted as he had at the hotel, she would fire him. Yes, she would. She would go on without him. Her hard-riding father had left her in control of everything—the ranch was clear, and she had enough money in the bank to establish a ranch in the valley. In that event, she suddenly sensed, she might sell out in Texas. It dawned on her that she really hadn't gone that far in her future planning until this moment. As in her loneliness she often turned to her mother's memory, she now sought the strength of her tough old dad. She hoped she had inherited enough of it to see her through.

Her four years at Mrs. Pettigrew's School for Young Ladies in St. Louis, with thankful summers on the ranch for relief from books and manners and proper dress for all occasions, had hardly prepared her for this. It burdened her how her father, a veteran of many clashes, had died so violently. Had he been ambushed? That didn't tally for Rip Holloway, a plainsman of his savvy and experience fighting off Comanche raiders and border riff-raff, both Mexican and Anglo. More likely, riding alone, as he often did, he had just been outgunned.

She realized sadly she would never know the details. It hurt her that he had died alone, except for faithful old Hondo, for which she was grateful. The *bandidos* had taken her father's rifle and six-gun. Why not Hondo?

On her return she passed a Mexican couple in a farm wagon headed downriver. They waved and smiled in a remembering way that pleased her, and she smiled and greeted them with: *"Buenos días."*

The day was still young when she reached the ford at the river crossing below Rosita. While Barney took his fill, she drank from the canteen and observed the eye-appealing grassy range stretching away to the mountains. She had plenty of time for another ride before dark; it was important, she thought, that she know the upper valley as well as the lower, where she had ventured today, and where Arch Kinder and the others were.

On that bent, she crossed the playful Mimbres and soon found a trail that ran dimly toward the mountains. Holding Barney to a steady trot, she gazed left and right. Before long she came to a log cabin, settling with age, and behind it an empty pole corral and shed. The cabin showed signs of recent repairs on the roof. There was a stack of split firewood. A pile of freshly cut poles out front could be preparation for new construction, maybe a porch or small room. *Somebody is determined to make a home of this old cabin,* she mused.

Onward past the cabin the trail played out, and she was of a mind to turn back when she came upon what looked like an old trail being cleared. Before taking it, she looked around to make certain of her bearings, then lightly touched spurs. The trail began to climb, and presently she was breathing cooler, pine-scented air and Barney was padding along on pine-needle footing. They moved along for some minutes.

Suddenly hearing the distinct *thunk* of an axe ahead of her, she pulled up. Soon after that she saw a white man emerge from timber along the trail. He saw her about the same time and gave her a friendly wave. Curious, she rode slowly toward him, wondering if she was about to see her first mountain man. Then she noticed a saddled horse by the trail.

"Good afternoon, Miss Holloway," he greeted her as she drew near. "I'm Evan Shelby."

"Oh, yes. How did you know it was me?"

"From the other day when you spoke at the meeting. And I believe you're the only young Anglo lady in Rosita at the moment. I hope I didn't startle you."

"You did surprise me. I approached you very carefully."

"As you should have. I apologize for causing you concern. When I saw you pull up, I waved to let you know it was all right to come ahead. What I'm doing here today is sort of renewing an old, old Indian trail, which I believe leads to the Black Range."

"Black Range?"

"North and northeast of us. Rugged country and beautiful, as you would imagine. Also, Indian country. . . . You know, Miss Holloway, you shouldn't be riding alone into these mountains."

"You say that, yet here you are clearing out a trail."

"True. I try to keep a look-out while I work, and I have a carbine on my saddle." He made a fruitless gesture. "If a war party came rushing down the trail, I'd probably get overrun, wouldn't I?"

"Unless you saw them coming."

He became amused. "And here I am warning you not to go into the mountains."

Her reply was a condoning smile. "I guess you feel you need to do this?"

"I do it to stay busy. I live not far from here. You must have passed that old cabin and the corral?"

"Rode right by it."

Besides the enjoyment of their conversation, he found himself wishing somehow to please her in his limited way. He discovered that her eyes were a deeper blue than he'd first thought. Her lips were softly cast, and, when she smiled, she revealed a sweet earnestness that was most appealing to him as a man, furthermore in a face so calmly pretty and natural. The sun brought a warm color to her cheeks. In her dark riding skirt and tan shirt and waves of light brown hair swept back under a gray hat, she completed quite a picture before him. *She can't be a day over nineteen or twenty,* he thought.

"I was just about to quit," he said. "Could you join me at the cabin for a late lunch? I baked a loaf of bread yesterday, my first. If you'd dare take the risk, I could fix you a bread-and-butter sandwich. I get butter from the valley . . . keep it fresh in a crock by the stream."

"Thank you, Mister Shelby, but I'd better not. I had a breakfast at Hannah Young's that would satisfy a hay hand. However, glad to ride with you."

"Fine. I know what you mean about Hannah's meals. She still thinks she's serving cowboys. I stayed there before I found the cabin." He stuck the handle of the axe in the carbine's sheath and mounted.

Nothing more was said as they rode side by side until the corral and cabin came into view. "Miss Holloway," he said, hoping to hold her a while longer, "if you have the time, I would like to show you my cook stove. Then maybe I can still talk you into having lunch."

"Your cook stove?" she said, with a slow smile.

"Yes. I'm sorta proud of that little stove. It has taught me how to cook. Or, I should say, has dared me to learn or go hungry."

"Well, if you're that proud of your stove, I must see it." She continued to smile as she spoke.

They tied up, and he opened the cabin door for her, and, as she entered, he said: "There it is . . . what keeps me from starving."

"It is small, isn't it?" she said, marveling a bit.

"Small . . . but cooks big. Heats up fast."

She sniffed. "I believe I can still smell your fresh bread, Mister Shelby. If your invitation still stands, I'll have a bread-and-butter sandwich."

Delighted, he performed an extravagant bow. "Your servant, Miss Holloway. You bet it stands. I'll be right back," he said, and went for the butter.

She noted that he kept a neat house and a clean kitchen. Over there his few books and newspapers on a shelf. A book of Tennyson's poems. His blue Army uniform looked brushed and clean. Twin bars on the shoulders. She wondered why Evan Shelby had come to the valley.

He fixed sandwiches. She complimented him on his bread, and afterward he said: "I liked what you said at the meeting the other day, Miss Holloway. It was well-stated. Sincere. Very friendly. . . . I fear my own remarks were misinterpreted by Mister Conklin. I wasn't trying to put a damper on things. I just wanted valley people to stop and think before they made any quick deals."

"You said the prices Mister Conklin quoted were far too low. What do you call fair prices?"

"Along the river and prime grazing, four to five dollars an acre. No less than three. Conklin said two. I'd say at least two for upland range. He said one. I guess it all comes down to how eager a man is to sell and if he needs the money. But when a man decides to sell his home place, he should think twice and get a fair price. You see, people here aren't used to sitting down and having to dicker, if that's the word. . . . That's my main concern."

"I see. You don't want anyone hurt. Well, I don't either."

"It's really none of my business," Evan said, passing it off. "I only stood up when nobody else did. After the meeting, folks came up and said they were glad I did."

"That's understandable, Mister Shelby. People need a voice."

"I appreciate your saying so. Not all your crew are of the same mind. A man named Code challenged me. Told me to stay out of this."

Alarm spread across her face. "That's Code Sloan, a new rider. He had no right to say that."

"It was after the meeting, in the saloon. I have to say he caught me by surprise."

"Surely there was no gun play?"

"Not a shot fired, I'm relieved to say. Hardly enough time for a man to get drunk and go that far."

She looked at him in a particular way. "What did you say to that?"

"I told him I intended to help valley people any way I could. Nothing more was said. Don't worry, Miss Holloway. I'm not going out of my way looking for trouble. Better, if I hadn't mentioned it."

"I'll speak to Arch Kinder about it."

"Don't. Just let it ride. It would look like I'm an informer, ran to you with it . . . when it just popped out of conversation. I feel it's strictly between Code Sloan and myself." His face crinkled into an understanding grin. "Sometimes men, like small boys, take a quick dislike for each other for no worthy reason." He wouldn't tell her about the incident of the carbine in front of the store. He'd just said enough here—too much, in fact.

Rising to leave, she gave him her hand. "I enjoyed the visit, and thank you very much for the unusual lunch . . . fresh bread and country butter. Had you not told me about the bread, I would have expected biscuits. I grew up on biscuits and cornbread, and tortillas, I should add."

"I'm not bad at biscuits. I enjoyed the visit, too. And I hope you get your ranch, Miss Holloway."

She paused at the doorway. "Having been around a Southern colonel or two who preferred to be addressed by rank . . . and you'd better not forget it, suh . . . I'm reminded that I should have addressed you as captain."

Seeing that she was serious, he nearly broke into laughter. "Oh, no. Plain Mister Shelby's just fine. Better still, just Evan. As I said at the meeting, I was a captain in the Union cavalry. Frankly, I wish we could all put the war behind us and any high-sounding reference to it."

He watched her mount and ride toward the river, his cavalryman's eye telling him that she rode with obvious ease. She made a man think of life beyond today. He supposed he should have told her he was a recovering lunger—there was no other way to put it—which would have explained his presence in the valley. But would he have sounded like a man seeking sympathy from a pretty young woman? He sure as hell didn't want that!

Just before she rode out of sight, she turned and flung him a cheery wave. He waved back, again and again, surprised and delighted, then she was gone. He hoped he saw her again.

She watered her horse at the river, in no mood to hurry through the lazy and enjoyable afternoon, her mind still lingering on Evan Shelby and his laughter about rank. He'd been very nice to her, a gentleman. She had to wonder why a man with his education and training chose to live in a lonely cabin.

Coming in on the road, she heard horsemen behind her, and saw Arch Kinder and Conklin and the riders.

Kinder spurred up beside her at once, flicking his glance across the river and back at her. His eyes questioned her.

"Cindy, you should never ride alone. You know that. And never across the river into the mountains."

It was the way he said it that stung her, as if he owned her. She looked straight at him. "I'm on a good horse and you see my Henry rifle, which I know how to use."

"You know what I mean," he said, easing off. "It's risky."

"It was a beautiful ride. I saw only one person, Captain Shelby." By now Conklin and the rest had caught up with them. "Did you-all sign up any landowners?" she asked, ignoring Kinder as she switched her attention to Conklin.

Conklin was slumped in the saddle, his round face the color of raw beef. It took him a moment to speak. "Everybody's holding back, waitin' for us to show up with bags of gold nuggets. I think it all goes back to that meeting and what that fella Shelby said. They won't budge from sky-high prices."

"That's right," Kinder seconded. "Somebody needs to talk sense into these people."

"We'll go upriver tomorrow," Conklin said. "Right now I need a drink."

She rode between them. When they reached town, Kinder drew her aside while the others headed for the Gem. "We need to talk," he said to her.

"About what?"

"About yesterday."

"I don't see why."

"Aw, come on, Cindy."

"Not today," she replied, and rode on to the livery, while he spurred for the saloon. She'd had an enjoyable day, the kind of ride that always lifted her up and cleared her mind. Why spoil it? Webb was there immediately to take her horse as she dismounted. "Thank you, Jim. Is Mister Brown here?" She refused to call this kind man Bear.

"I'm right here," said a cordial voice from the office door. "What can I do for you, Miss Holloway?"

"I like Barney very much. Would you consider parting with him?"

"Well . . . might," Brown said, coming out.

He was a cagey horse trader, she sensed that, and she said: "I worked him out pretty good. He has the nicest running walk. Handles well. Doesn't shy every time a bird flies out of a bush."

"He's a good horse."

"Once I dismounted and dropped the reins to see what he would do. He just stood there . . . looking at me and around. Never moved away. I walked off a little way, and he still never moved. Just watched me. In fact, he seemed kind of curious as to what I was up to. If he'd taken off, it would have been a long walk back to Rosita."

"He's ranch-broke."

"That certainly shows. We got along fine. But I fear he's a little on the old side at eight." She was beginning to dicker, as her father and Hap McCoy had taught her.

"Just right for these mountains. Ride a horse too hard in up-and-down country before he matures, you can break him down. That goes for four and five-year-olds. Not every horse grows at the same rate. A horse needs time to develop and build up."

"How much do you want for Barney, Mister Brown?"

He gazed up at a rafter. "Reckon I might let him go for two hundred."

She showed him a subtle look. "*Pesos* or dollars?"

His smile widened. "Dollars, Miss Holloway."

She rocked back and forth a little. "As good a horse as Barney is, I'd have to think about that, Mister Brown." You never took the first offer.

"How would a hundred and seventy-five sound to you?"

"Better, but. . . ."

All at once, wishing very much to please her, he gave in and said: "You can have Barney for one-fifty. And I'll throw in a new bridle, silver-mounted, and new blanket. Even have him fresh-shod. What do you say, Miss Holloway?"

She felt a rush of appreciation. "I'd say that's very generous of you, Mister Brown. Thank you, sir. I shall take Barney. You are very obliging to me, a stranger."

He took her quick hand. "You're no stranger here. I told Bear this morning you were well brought up."

"Ranch-broke, like Barney," she said, smiling. "My father did the best he could." The kindness here touched her deeply. "I'd like to stall Barney here."

"We'll sure take care of him for you, you bet. And all your gear."

Webb was already unsaddling Barney.

She gave Barney a pat and strolled to the hotel, feeling completely fulfilled. Today she had made new friends and she had a good mountain horse.

Chapter Five

Pablo Garza was at Evan Shelby's cabin door not long after breakfast. Instead of walking, he came by mule, which indicated unusual haste.

"What brings you here so early, Pablo? How about some coffee? I was just wondering how I should go about building a little porch. Or maybe a *ramada?*"

"I would like the coffee, *amigo* Evan, thank you. But do nothing about the porch now. I weel help you later." He looked despairingly at the pile of poles. "Do not even think about a *ramada*. The brush roof would leak, and you would be an unhappy man."

"Better for the desert, eh?"

"Yes."

"What's up?" Evan asked over coffee.

"You are invited to leetle meeting at my house this afternoon. A few neighbors are thinking about selling out. They don't know what to do. They ask me. I tell them . . . 'Don't rush into anything.' But they keep thinking about money. They need to talk to somebody else. I am just Pablo, their old neighbor."

"Are you and Josefa thinking about selling?"

"She would heet me over the head if I said one word. Where would we go? Here I can feed my family, and we have a good school."

"That's a good way to look at it, Pablo. The valley will grow as more and more people hear about it. Before many years the valley will be in a county and there will be an election for county officials . . . a sheriff and a judge and an attorney to prosecute for crimes. There'll be an office where a landowner like you can go and put his property on record and have a deed to show for it . . . that way nobody can ride in and take it away from him. . . . Your land will become more valuable as more people come in. Also, you will begin to pay taxes on your land and house."

Garza grimaced. "Taxes? I wouldn't like that."

Evan laughed knowingly. "Nobody likes taxes. But all property owners will pay some taxes. You won't go broke. Taxes will be needed to run the county . . . to pay the officials. One town will have all the county offices. It will be called the county seat."

"Could that be Rosita?"

"I suppose so. Or maybe a town where they have gold and silver, like Piños Altos." Evan stopped short. "Now what could I do at your meeting? I don't own any land. I just live in this cabin."

"You were the only one who stood up at the schoolhouse. They weel listen to you."

"Why don't you all sit down and let everybody have his say?"

Garza grinned. "We have done that."

"Well, that's a start."

"But nothing happened. We need somebody not Mexican to talk to us, and maybe guide us. Make us see everything. You are educated man, *amigo* Evan. A man from the outside. A United States *capitán* in the beeg *Americano* war. Before that you fought Apaches along the Río Grande."

Evan said nothing.

"Before that you went to beeg military school. One time you told me."

"West Point. I am a graduate."

Garza pointed a forefinger. "That is what I mean. You are graduate man. So come to meeting. Let your voice be heard. I promise you we weel listen."

"All right, Pablo. I will for you and Josefa."

"And later I weel help you with your porch."

"You've already done too much."

"I would call it a beginning, *amigo*. Come early this afternoon."

Instead of Garza's "leetle meeting" of "a few neighbors," Evan rode up to a yard crowded with saddle horses. His friend was waiting for him at the door, wearing a guilty grin that asked forgiveness.

"More people showed up than expected after I passed the word you would be here," he said.

"You rascal," Evan said, poking him in the shoulder. "Judging from the number of horses here, you didn't just pass the word *after* you talked to me . . . you did before. You knew I couldn't turn you down."

Garza's answer was to seek silent forgiveness and to open the door and graciously invite Evan in. Josefa was waiting, looking excited and pleased. "We weel have a nice dinner after the meeting, *Señor* Evan."

"It couldn't be otherwise at your house, Josefa," he said.

Garza took over the meeting and asked who would speak first and explain the situation. A gray-haired man, diffident and quite thin and tired-looking, held up his hand.

"You, Benito Otero. Fine."

"No," Otero said, raising veined hands, "I don't speak too good. Could you speak for me, Pablo? You know how everything is with me."

"I weel try."

"*Gracias.* I much want *Señor* Shelby to hear."

"Benito's parents in California," Garza began slowly, "are getting on in years. They are too old to be moved here. His dear wife, Amelia, passed away last year. We all remember." Heads were nodding. "Apaches killed Arturo, his only son, three years ago. His daughter, Elena, is married and living in Santa Fé."

Garza glanced at Otero, as if to say—"Am I telling this right?" And got an emphatic nod of approval.

"Benito thinks it is time for him to leave the Mimbres, though he weel always remember eet. Life has been good most times. He feels he must go take care of his parents, who brought him up in hard times. He thinks he himself will feel better near the ocean . . . the salt air." He glanced again at Otero, who nodded, and Garza went on. "He has five hundred acres of good range and some farm land. There is also a nice orchard. He had farmed the lower part, near the river. Eet could be turned back to pasture easy enough." Garza took a long breath. "Empire has offered him two dollars an acre, which Benito has refused." Then, turning to Evan: "Do you think he was wise to turn down the offer?"

"Yes. That's not enough money. He needs to rock back and forth, talk to them again. But don't appear too eager to sell."

"Benito says eet is hard to talk to these people. They are not gracious like valley people. This lawyer man called Conklin . . . the beeg fat one . . . got in Benito's face and talked loud. With him was the man called Kinder, who was not friendly . . . stared hard at Benito all the time. Benito was by himself at the house. So he feel uneasy and questioned his judgment."

"What happened after *Señor* Otero turned down their offer?"

Garza looked at Otero. They exchanged rapid Spanish.

The older man appeared concerned. Then Garza looked at Evan. "Conklin said that was their last offer . . . for Benito to think about eet. If he wants to talk about eet again, to leave word at the land office in town. They rushed out of the house and rode off fast. Benito say they make him think of border outlaws he saw as a young *vaquero* in Chihuahua."

"Did they ever threaten him in any way?" Evan asked.

"No. Eet was their manner . . . how they talk and act."

"Threat enough. That's an old trick, telling a man that's their final offer . . . and tearing off, trying to make Benito think he's letting a good deal slip through his fingers. They were rushing Benito. You seldom take the first offer in any transaction. When did this happen?"

"Day before yesterday. What do you think Benito should do now?"

"I'd say wait a few days. Don't appear too eager to sell. Then ride in . . . say he'll parley again at his place. When they come out, which they will because they want the land, try for three dollars an acre. Stand fast. Don't take much less. I think they'll come up a little." He looked at Otero in a sympathetic way. "In the long run, it all depends how important it is for Benito to do this."

"What if he waits a long time and they don't come back?"

"Whatever a person does, he shouldn't sell for less than what he thinks he has is worth. Unless he's desperate."

"Benito is not desperate yet."

Garza and Otero traded more fast Spanish. After which Garza, displaying another of his forgive-me expressions, turned to Evan and said: "Benito thanks you for your wise words and now wishes to ask a great favor of you, *amigo* Evan, *Capitán* Evan. Most hopefully, he does."

Warily Evan asked: "What is it?"

"He respectfully asks you to represent him the next time

he talks to these hard *gringos.*"

"But I'm not a lawyer, and I guess I'm also considered a *gringo.*"

"You are Anglo, but you are not *gringo* . . . you are *amigo.* You don't understand what we Mexicans mean when we say *gringo.*" He drew his face into an ugly scowl and pushed out his lower lip in a manner that made Evan grin.

"I'm glad I'm not that," Evan chuckled, "but I'm still not a lawyer."

"There's not a lawyer in the whole valley. What Benito needs is for somebody to be with him . . . to give him strength . . . since he has no family."

"How about you, Pablo? You're a good talker."

That brought endorsing snickers all around.

"Well, maybe a little, sometimes," Garza admitted sheepishly, and then in a serious vein, he said: "It will help a Mexican to have an Anglo *capitán* from the beeg *Americano* war on his side."

Evan was frowning. He did not want to appear unfeeling or without understanding of a good man's problems. And so, with some hesitation, he replied: "I will help if I can," knowing he might be drawn into something he couldn't handle. "I will be there to back you up, Benito. Let me know when. However, since you're the landowner, you'll have to do most of the talking. I hope I can help in some way, if nothing more than providing an ear for your comments on the side and for someone you can confer with about an offer."

Benito Otero jumped up. "Oh, *gracias, señor. Gracias.*"

"I don't know where your place is," Evan said.

"I weel show you . . . a few miles up the river."

Chapter Six

Lucinda Holloway was growing more restless by the day. It would be a while before Hap McCoy could be here. She had seen Arch Kinder and Conklin and the riders going and returning, always heading for the Gem. They seemed to spend a lot of time there. The crew was out again this morning. She had managed to avoid seeing Arch alone since that one time, instead, talking business at the office. Thus far Empire had been able to purchase only three ranches, the last, four hundred acres south of Rosita from a white man bent on going to Oregon. He had sold out for two dollars an acre. Both Arch and Conklin were showing signs of temper at the slow sales. In all honesty, she didn't want a Texas-size ranch in this gentle valley. When she had sufficient range and water for a thousand head or so, she would call it off, which she knew would shock Conklin, a promoter, and anger Arch, with his visions of another Empire spread in New Mexico, with him as *segundo*.

It occurred to her that she must have inherited much of her father's driving purpose, because at the thought she was soon dressed for riding and at the livery asking Webb for her horse.

"Good morning, Miss Holloway," Webb greeted her. "None of my business, but where would you be headin' for today?"

"South a way, then across the river."

"I know it ain't polite to speak up like this, but you should be mighty careful. Always stay alert. Look all around you all the time. Pull up at any movement. If in doubt, turn ol' Barney for home."

"The same held true in Texas, only you could see farther," she said blithely.

He felt he had to say more. "For years I trapped and hunted in the mountains. Made it, except for the one time I chanced on a grizzly. Twice, small parties of Apaches came for me. Only I knew the country better than they did . . . because I lived there and moved mostly on foot. Not all of 'em got back to their camps in the Black Range. So mighty early I learned always to look around . . . an' listen sharp . . . before I went ahead. You do the same now." He made a quick gesture of apology. " 'Nuff said. Know you will."

"Thank you, Jim. I promise I'll do that."

"Ma'am, why don't you call me Bear? Everybody does. It don't bother me a-tall."

"Then Bear it is. Thank you."

"An' if you need any help, just let ol' Bear know. I'm not as helpless as I might look."

"Thank you. You are very kind, you and Mister Brown."

"Silas will be sorry he missed you. He's at the Gem for his morning phlegm-cutter."

Barney was eager, and she let him out after a short way, and he stepped into his ground-eating running walk. Soon, coming to the ford, she reined up and watched the Mimbres, listening to its shushing song over gravel, while Barney took his fill. A mountain horse, she thought, would never turn down a drink.

They crossed at a walk, and she struck out for Evan Shelby's cabin, knowing that had been her destination from the start. Why, she didn't quite know: instinct, mood, restlessness, loneliness, the need to get about from having been brought up on a working ranch. She'd been low since her father's death, and would be, she knew, until she had acquired enough range to establish his dream ranch, which would be a tribute to him and his memory, a symbol of the peace he'd never had. He had not revealed as much to her, but she sensed that he had grown weary of the continual struggle in Texas. Had he, she wondered, also envisioned the ranch for her, away from the same violence-torn life?

Evan Shelby was saddling when she rode up. He looked at her with pleased surprise. "Miss Holloway! A little earlier and I would have offered you breakfast, with some of my unforgettable biscuits. Meaning, that could be taken either of two ways . . . edible or better try cornbread next time."

"Out for a little ride, hoping I might find you before you left to work on the trail."

"My pleasure. No trail labor today. Some time ago I was out, sort of exploring, and came across a beautiful little spring in high country. It's actually a votive spring. I'd like to show it to you. Can you be gone that long? Will promise to get you back here well before dark."

"I have plenty of time. Hannah packed me a lunch. As one would expect, it's enough for two people."

"And I have mine. Let's go."

He led off at a trot, and presently they came in on the ancient trace he was restoring and followed it some distance. After a reckoning look around, he reined away, and they began a gradual ascent, working back and forth through a woodland of *piñon* pines and juniper and afterward stands of aspen and ponderosa pines. She noticed that he continuously scanned about them. Now and then he halted for another reckoning and rested the horses. The air was bracing. The squeak of saddle leather and the soft padding of hoofs on the pine-needle floor the only sounds of their passage, she at his side.

They started across a pretty meadow. Nearby a little band

of does with yellowish-brown fawns alertly took notice and, moving like smoke, gradually faded into the timber, dissolving into shadows.

"Oh, my," she said, spellbound. "Like magic, they're gone."

He waited until there was nothing more to see, then he turned his horse and said: "It's not far now."

She hadn't thought about time, absorbed as she was with all that was passing before her.

Now he took them on an angling, horse-grunting climb, then along the base of a low cliff with a broad face of smooth rock set off from a scattering of pines standing like sentinels.

"There it is," he said, checking. "Below the cliff. Out a little way. Hear it?"

She saw the glittering pool of a jewel-like spring in the dappled light. To her, in the stillness, its murmuring as sweet as any song. The sight and the sound held them both. She was filled with pleasure, entranced.

"I wanted you to see it first in the broken light through the pines," he said. "Let's water the horses below the spring. It overflows enough to form a pool a little way down and eventually becomes a small branch. Not enough for a creek, but it never stops."

They watered the horses and led them back and tied them close at hand.

"Now," he said, taking her hand, "you will see why this is a special place," and took her around broken footing to a flat rock that overlooked the spring. "Now kneel and look down," he said, kneeling first.

She looked down, then, leaning lower, suddenly exclaimed: "They look like black arrowheads . . . and I see blue and green stones! The stones are beautiful."

"The arrowheads are obsidian and the blue and green

stones are turquoise. Also, down there are some beads and pottery shards." He reached down and brought up a streaming handful of arrowheads for her to see. She picked one up, as curious as a child. He reached down again, searching, guided by his eyes, and scooped up several pieces of turquoise for her to examine. One dark-blue stone was a perfect half moon.

"These must have been offerings," he said. "A veneration of water, which makes sense in an arid land. Here, take this half-moon blue stone as a keepsake."

She looked at it for moments, admiring it; however, instead of taking it, as he assumed she would, she shook her head, and, smiling softly, handed it back, saying: "These have to be heartfelt offerings, they're so beautiful. But it wouldn't be right to take another person's offering, even if it was long ago." She gazed up at the turquoise sky. "This place is truly special. I understand why you wanted to come back here, Evan, and show it to me. It's like a shrine with holy water."

Her sensitivity overwhelmed him, left him speechless for the moment. She was so appealing and sincere, so utterly honest and endearing, qualities that moved him. He found his voice. "I understand how you feel, and respect you for it. I just wanted you to have something extra beautiful and unusual . . . that isn't commonly found." Her deep-blue eyes met his, locked, and then each looked away. "I believe I can predict what will happen here as the valley settles up and more people ride into these mountains," he said in a matter-of-fact voice. "Someday, by chance, a rider will discover this blessed place as I did. And when he waters his horse and kneels down to drink, he'll see the arrowheads and trove of beautiful stones, and he'll scoop up all he can . . . especially the turquoise . . . throw it all in a greasy sack and ride off to the settlements, where he'll trade it for whisky." He shook his head and changed his tone. "I hope I'm wrong. Now, I want to show you a cave these long-ago people called home, then let's eat lunch. What do you say, Miss Holloway?"

"I'm all for it, sir," she answered in a voice as light as his.

The cave was at the foot of the cliff a short walk from the spring. Thinking of bears, he approached warily. But it didn't look deep enough for a hibernating grizzly; in fact, it was rather shallow.

Again he took her hand, and, standing together, they peered in at the smoke-blackened walls and at the stick-like figures carved above the entrance.

"I take it the figures represent warriors," she said after a bit. "That drawing on the end, the larger one, is that a snake?"

"A plumed serpent, maybe," he said as thoughtfully. "I feel guilty for not knowing more about the Mimbres and the early people. A man needs to order some books. But since most of this man's life has been spent on horseback at war, he finds himself limited by his almost total ignorance." Of course, talking to her, he had left out the time he'd spent searching for a cure.

She looked at him. "You're hard on yourself, Captain. There was no time for anything else then."

"And lucky if you got through it. I was lucky. But later you see what you'd missed."

"There's still time to catch up a little."

She made him smile. "That has occurred to me."

A breeze ran whimpering along the face of the cliff. They had hardly moved. A raven fussed at them from the lightning-blasted crown of a ponderosa.

"I've wondered why these hardy people vanished, and where they went and why," Evan mused. "Maybe invaders drove them out . . . or there was a long drought. Although they had plenty of wood and water, life must have been hard. They could hunt deer and gather *piñon* nuts and plant corn and melons and squash and beans along the river. You wonder if they ever ventured south out on the desert . . . end of this man's know-nothing lecture. Time we took a peek inside the cave."

The dimensions of the cave were even less than Evan had thought from a distance. It extended only about ten feet from the entrance.

She hugged herself and hesitated. "I don't like caves."

"I don't either, much . . . stay here." He went inside, talking back to her as he looked around. "I was hoping maybe we'd see a basket or a bowl . . . some stone tools or a *metate* to grind corn on or nuts. But it's been so long ago here. I don't see anything."

He looked down and brushed at something on the floor with a forefinger. More curious, he opened his pocketknife and picked at the object. It flipped up. He held it and rubbed it and came out wearing a little smile of triumph, saying— "Here's something you can keep that's not an offering."— and held out a rounded piece of turquoise as blue as the sky.

Her mouth fell. She rubbed it gently and held it up to the light. "It's beautiful," she said. "Oh, thank you, Evan . . . oh, my, I never saw turquoise until today. It's such a touching thing."

"I wanted you to have something from here. Won't it make a pendant, say? It's too big for a ring."

"Oh, yes . . . a pendant. It's so lovely. Thank you again." She gazed at the cave, then up at the perfect sky. "From these ancients. The Forgotten Ones. Somehow they still feel near. Watching. Yet not minding. Because we, like them, are only temporary residents."

"Like gentle ghosts, they are," he mused. "Well spoken, Lucinda."

They drifted back to the spring in thoughtful silence.

"We haven't yet had a drink from the votive spring," he said. "Be sure to take off your hat."

She darted him a look. "Believe I do know enough to do that, Captain Shelby," she rebuked him gently. "How else do you think a Texan could learn to drink out of cow tracks during a drought?"

He uttered a quick laugh, struck by his own absurdity. "I didn't mean that you're a little girl and had to be told."

"Do I act like one?" she challenged him.

"Not at all. You could ride for my old cavalry unit right now. However, I'd have to check your marksmanship with pistol and Spencer carbine and see how you handle a saber before I'd enlist you."

"Sorry, Captain. Wrong army. I'm a Confederate."

"At this point, the honorable Captain Shelby, formerly brevet Major Shelby, surrenders and hands over his saber, unable to extricate himself from certain defeat."

"Surrender accepted, Captain. You and your men may keep your horses and take them home. You'll need them, plowing the fields and riding after milk cows."

Evan scratched his chin, feigning puzzlement. "Wasn't it Grant who said something like that at Appomattox?"

In turn, she put a pondering forefinger to her chin and said: "We Rebs never admit defeat."

And he rescued her further with: "At any rate, you are generous, suh. I'll think of you when I gather the corn crop this fall."

Smiling as she removed her hat, she brushed at her light-brown hair, knelt, and spread her hands for support and drank.

"It's icy cold," she exclaimed.

"Comes from the base of the cliff," he said.

They sat on the flat rock by the pool and ate lunch, listening to bird song and watching hawks circling for prey. A raven was back in the splintered ponderosa, as if to remind them they were unwelcome intruders. Evan thought she was enjoying the day, a release from being cooped up at the hotel amid Empire's unfinished business.

After a while, wishing they could stay longer, he looked at the sliding sun and said: "Believe we'd better get back. Don't want Hannah Young to be standing on her verandah, hands on hips, waiting for you."

"She's been very nice to me."

"You're in good hands."

She turned to look at the cave, her eyes lingering. "Glad you brought me to your special place. It's like going to church in the wildwood. So peaceful and giving."

"Without some arm-waving preacher shouting sin and damnation and stomping up dust around the pulpit, sweat pouring off his face. As a boy in church, I experienced such group tongue-lashings more than once and wished I was anywhere else. Preferably on a shaded creek bank with my old dog and my fishing pole."

They took the horses down to the pool, mounted there, and rode off. Evan was watchful as before, as was she, although she said no word, feeling relaxed and content.

The return ride seemed to pass unusually fast, she thought, when they reached the trail he was clearing off.

"I wanted to see if I could bring us back to the same point of departure we took off from," he said, frowning.

"Did you?"

"Only a Johnny Reb would ask that of a renowned Yankee guide who knows every bypath in these vast mountains."

"Well, did you, sir?" She was teasing him, knowing the answer.

"Not quite. In fact, Miss Holloway, we're about half a mile west of where we left."

"Oh, my. A terrible miscalculation. But in view of the fact that you managed to lead us to the most unusual and special place I've ever been, I believe your missed reckoning can be excused this one time, Captain Shelby, formerly brevet major."

"You are generous. A man always appreciates a last-second reprieve, ma'am."

At the cabin she declined his invitation to come in, and thanked him again and shook hands. "I hope I can have the blue stone made into a pendant, maybe next time I'm in El Paso."

"Silver would look good." He had been considering a matter while they rode back, and he said: "An older land-owner, *Señor* Benito Otero, has been talking to your Empire reps about selling his place, but no agreement reached. He has asked me to sit in with him when he talks again to Mister Conklin and Mister Kinder. I didn't particularly want to, but said I would help. He is not at ease talking to Anglos about money. . . . He came to the valley years ago from Mexico. His wife has died, and he has no family left here. He's decided to sell out and move to California and care for his parents . . . I thought perhaps you might be there, listening in?" The last was pure gamble, another chance to see her.

Surprise flicked across her face. "You must be peeking into my mind. I've been thinking that, as Empire's owner, I should be going on some of the calls to landowners. I shall make a point to be there. When is it and where is the ranch?"

"Benito is to let me know when. He has to tell the office in town when he's ready to parley again. His place is upriver."

She nodded. "I'll be there." She started to mount. Instead, she hesitated, reins in hand, and swung around and brushed him a kiss on the cheek, mounted, and rode off fast.

My Lord, he thought, struck dumb with amazement.

She left the cabin with the sense that she would return soon. Evan Shelby had been very nice to her, considerate of her in every way. She liked him. She adored the turquoise. She had enjoyed being with him and talking to him; the back-and-forth banter had been fun. Furthermore, he had made her laugh, and she needed the tonic of laughter. And they hadn't exchanged one differing word about the War Between the States, which she knew he would have referred to in another way, yet without offending her. The entire day still pulsed within her. He had taken her to a place of reverence and mystery. Everything remained inscribed on her mind, not to be forgotten, like the ancient figures above the cave. . . . She wondered about Evan. Why was he here, living such a lonely life? Apparently, he had given up a military career. Why? He hadn't mentioned a family, not anyone. He was not a sad man; he was a happy man, although he must be lonely at times. Could he be a fugitive, on the dodge from something back East? She dismissed the thought; it didn't fit the man. He was too open and at ease. She might ask Hannah.

At the turn in the trail, she looked back and waved, sensing he would be watching her—he was. And he waved, and he was still waving when she went on. He stayed in her thoughts as she rode.

A blur of subtle movement in the trees across the river broke into her reflections and caught her eyes. A solitary horseman. He did not move. He was looking her way. Of a sudden she had the uneasy feeling that she was being observed. In another moment the rider vanished. She reined up, watching. He was gone from sight. He did not reappear. At least, he wasn't an Apache. She was sure of that. Maybe just a passing rider. Casting aside her concern, she continued on to the river, let Barney take a long drink.

When she came out on the road to town, there was no one, and the fullness of the day returned to her.

Chapter Seven

That morning, in advance of the afternoon meeting with Empire's reps, Evan rode with Benito Otero over his land and found the range abundant with grama grass and the lower section along the river well-suited for farming. The orchard showed early promise. Otero said he had plans for irrigation if he couldn't sell. He had done very little since the death of his dear wife, selling off most of his cattle, content to get by with a little farming. It didn't take much for one old Mexican, he said sadly.

"I'll stand by your side, if needed," Evan assured him. "Don't hold back. Don't be afraid. You have a nice ranch, and there is land for farming. Empire wants what you have."

"*Gracias, Señor* Evan."

"Don't worry. You just meet them at the door and invite them in. Hold out for three dollars an acre as long as you can."

Shortly after one o'clock Empire arrived in a pounding rush, Lucinda Holloway in front with Kinder and Conklin, followed by ten riders. Evan recognized Code Sloan, swaggering even in the saddle. A tough-looking crew, as Otero had said at Pablo's.

Miss Holloway was very attractive in her riding outfit. She was smiling and gave the impression of anticipation. He hoped her being here meant no rough tactics. Not doubting she would take part, he could feel a mounting interest in what lay ahead.

Señor Otero might not have the grandiose manner of a *hacendado,* Evan saw, but he appeared to take a grip on himself and was genuinely friendly and courteous by the time he went to the door and held it open and invited in the two negotiators and Miss Holloway. The crew, looking bored, began lounging on the verandah.

Otero gestured toward a table with five chairs. Evan was standing. When the three were seated, Otero and Evan took chairs. Miss Holloway smiled at Evan. He nodded and smiled his evident pleasure. She was, indeed, an engaging young woman, more to her than her appealing prettiness. Declining the turquoise offering from the votive spring had not only surprised him, but had revealed an unusual sensitivity and regard for others. He had turned that over in his mind more than once.

Kinder, openly displeased at the change of line-up, laid a blunt stare on Evan that carried the unmistakable question: *What the hell are you doing here?*

To ease the situation, Evan said: "I'm a friend of *Señor* Otero's. He asked me to sit in with him. Sometimes he has a little trouble with his English." In other words, Evan was telling them, I'm here to see that this old Mexican gets a fair deal. "He has a nice spread, and there is also farming. I've been over it with him."

Kinder said nothing, but still didn't like it. He glanced at Conklin, who briefly reviewed his notes. And then, with a persuasive smile for Otero, he said: "It is good to see you again, *Señor* Otero. We of Empire hope you've had enough time to consider the generous offer we left with you?"

"You mean, *señor,* the two dollars an acre?"

"Yes."

"I have thought about that, *señor,*" Otero began in a halting voice. "I cannot sell my ranch for that. Eet is not enough. Thees land below the mountains is too dear to me. . . . I have cared for eet many years. Never overgraze.

There is no better range in all the valley."

Conklin smiled expansively. "We understand how you feel this way about your ranch, *Señor* Otero. It has been your life. You are close to it every day. You have cared for it well. However, what we quoted you is the fair market price for good range all over New Mexico, including the Río Grande, and up north, and in northeastern New Mexico, where the ranch country stretches out toward the plains. In fact, much of that land can be bought right now for as low as a dollar an acre." He paused to make the point. "I was told that in Las Cruces on the way out here." The disarming smile returned. "And remember, *Señor* Otero, we are talking about money on the barrelhead, as the old saying goes. When you agree to sell your ranch, you will get your money immediately at *Señor* Keeley's. . . . That's all there is to it. No wrangle. No delay. Now what do you say, *Señor* Otero?"

Without looking at Evan for support, the old Mexican shook his head, unmoved.

Conklin's confident manner did not change. "Friends don't always agree at first. And what do friends do when they don't? They talk some more as we are doing now. For that reason, I point out to you there's plenty of free range south of the Mimbres Valley, on down past the Florida Mountains. We could take that for nothing. There's a huge spring at the end of the Mimbres Mountains called Cooke's Spring, and the river flows on west of the spring."

Otero's shrug as much as said: *"Then why not take eet?"*

Conklin was quick. "Because the valley has more to offer. Much more, *señor*."

"True," the old man said. "I can tell you why. I have been horseback over the free land you talk about. Cooke's Spring, beeg as eet is, could not water a herd of cattle spread over many miles." He smiled. "And the river dies at north end of the Floridas . . . goes underground . . . disappears in an alkali flat. I have been there, *señor*."

The old man's got him, Evan said to himself.

"You could," Otero went on, as if wishing to be helpful, "put up many windmills for stock water . . . but very expensive."

Conklin flushed a deep red. "Well stated, *señor*. Why we prefer the valley. Why Empire is offering you a fair price. Think it over." He waited several moments, then: "What do you say?"

Not hesitating, Otero replied: "*Señor,* with all respect, I cannot sell my land for two dollars. Three dollars eet is worth."

Conklin looked at Kinder. At an agreed signal, perhaps, both got up to leave.

Miss Holloway's quick voice checked them. "Can't we talk to *Señor* Otero some more? We just got here." There was a trace of irritation in her voice.

They sat back down, looking at her in stunned surprise. *Or,* Evan wondered, *was that an agreed on ploy to pressure the old man to make him come down? She playing the rôle of the peacemaker?* On second thought, he didn't think she would do it. Artifice was not her way.

"What do you suggest, Miss Holloway?" Conklin asked, miffed.

"Let's horse trade a little, as my father used to say." She turned to Otero. "Maybe we can beat that, *señor*. Maybe not," she said, smiling all the way.

That broke the stalemate. Smiling in return, Otero said: "Maybe, yes, *señorita*. *Gracias*. I listen, you talk to this old man of the valley."

"Would you listen to two dollars and a half per acre?"

He rolled his black eyes. He was enjoying this now, Evan

saw. A pretty girl could calm the waters fast.

Otero said: "I am listening, *señorita*. I do not want to make you feel sad . . . you are so *muy* nice. But, you see, I cannot sell my land for that." He was speaking very carefully and respectfully.

She regarded her reps. "I've never seen *Señor* Otero's ranch. I'd like to ride over it and see for myself. It shouldn't take long."

"No need to," Kinder said abruptly. "I've looked it over."

A tight silence rose between them, the ranch foreman ignoring the wishes of the young and spirited owner of Empire. Actually putting her down in front of others. Kinder sure of his place, a kind of confident arrogance about him. Evan caught it all.

Instead of flaring back at him, she nearly laughed, saying: "You must not have heard me clearly, Arch. I wish to ride over *Señor* Otero's spread. See it from the back of a good horse. And that is what we will do."

"Just tryin' to save us a little time," Kinder quickly backed off, his bold features flushing. "Shore, that's what we'll do, Miss Cindy."

"Fine. Let's go."

Conklin hid a half smile behind his left hand.

Señor Otero broke out into a broad smile.

Evan grinned, thinking: *Rip Holloway's daughter. Good for her!* Kinder would dominate her, if he could. As foreman of Empire, he likely stood to gain a great deal personally if he ran everything. She might give in a little, because she was generous, but she would not be forced against her will. He was proud of her spirit. Growing up among rough men in dangerous times, knowing how to talk to men, she seemed more mature than her youthful years. In the short time of their friendship, he had also sensed an unspoken loneliness that bothered him. As for Kinder, Evan didn't like the man or his roughshod ways, as just then demonstrated. Evan could only see trouble looming ahead for her in coming days.

They mounted and crossed the river and rode north, Otero next to Miss Holloway, Evan following with Kinder. Conklin had begged off to remain with the riders.

As Otero pointed them toward the mountains, she eagerly took notice of the pasture, empty of cattle. "The grass looks very good," she said, after an eye-sweeping assessment. "I'm used to short-grass country." She drew rein. "This grows in big bunches or patches. What is it called, *señor?*"

"Here you see both blue grama and side-oats grama. My cows loved eet. Side-oats grows up to three feet. Grama grasses cure well. In Texas you have buffalo grass, a short grass."

She had made him feel at ease. He had spoken graciously.

Dismounting, Otero plucked a handful of side-oats and passed it to her. She inspected it with close interest, a true daughter of the range, Evan thought. She rubbed several blades between her fingers, then slowly chewed on one.

"I can see how a hungry cow would like this," she said, smiling at Otero, who looked pleased. "It tastes good."

Evan had to tease her a trifle. "Exactly how does it taste, Miss Holloway?"

"Like good grass should, Captain Shelby," she flung back at him, and rode ahead.

Her pertness made him chuckle. Kinder did not laugh. His eyes on Evan contained the same bluntness as at the house—that Evan had no place in any of this and should stay out of it.

Then, not to be left out, Kinder spurred up beside her, saying: "Any pasture looks good if it hasn't been grazed for a season. Didn't you sell off some time ago, *señor?*"

"True, *Señor* Kinder. A small herd. But I have never

grazed my range too hard," he said with deep sincerity. "Eet takes more than one season for eet to recover if overgrazed."

Riding on, Otero halted them where the forest began.

"It's beautiful up here," Miss Holloway said.

"What about panthers and bears during the calving season?" Kinder asked, on the same critical line. "Didn't you lose calves?"

"Over the years I lost a few head. Not many. When the calves started dropping, I rode armed and moved my cows closer to the river. Panthers prefer deer meat," the old man explained. "There are plenty deer for them to hunt in the mountains . . . closer to their haunts. Bears have not bothered much. Too many people along the river."

From there he showed them the orchard, which he said covered two acres.

"Bears like apples," he said. "I have found them up in my trees, juice running down their hairy faces."

"What did you do?" Miss Holloway asked.

"I tried to shoo them away. Make beeg noise. Much shouting. Most times that worked. One time . . . only one time . . . I shot a bear. He was eating too many apples. Two days he eat my apples. He was about to ruin my crop. So I shot him. My dear wife, Amelia, was very unhappy. Better, almost, I let the bear have all the apples, she was so unhappy with me."

"You had to save your crop," she assured him. "Do you make apple cider?"

He looked down, in admission. "I used to. *Muy* good, I was told."

"If you hadn't shot the bear, there'd have been no cider that year."

He beamed. "That's what my friends said."

No more was said the rest of the way to the ranch. Evan

sensed that the sale was negotiable on either side, except for Kinder, who had positioned himself by his ranch owner's side with a possessive air.

At the house Otero invited everyone in with words and gestures, and they sat down as before as Conklin joined them.

"Well, *Señor* Otero," Lucinda began, "I said I would horse trade a little, and I intend to do that. I like your place. Good grass. Good water. Your adobe house has been well cared for, and could be extended on either side. Therefore, I offer you two dollars and seventy-five cents an acre."

Kinder and Conklin traded surprised looks.

Otero's face brightened, then changed back. "Pardon, *señorita*. I want to talk to my friend, *Señor* Shelby."

"Go ahead, *señor*."

Evan and Otero went to a corner, and the old man asked: "Should I take the *señorita's* offer?"

Evan chewed his lower lip. "Do what you think is fair and best for you."

"Eet is much better than two dollars, but I am stubborn. I still want three dollars."

"Then tell her that."

"*Señorita,*" Otero said, with great courtesy, "I thank you for your kind offer, but I still stand by three dollars."

"*Señor,*" she said, giving him a reminding smile, "I have come up from our original offer of two dollars an acre . . . that is a long way. I want you to be happy . . . to have enough money to take with you to California." Now she waited, kindness for him in her eyes.

"I still want three dollars, *señorita*."

"I know," she said in an understanding way.

Evan supposed it was her touching consideration for him that suddenly caused Otero to break into a broad smile and say, won over: "I accept your offer, *Señorita* Holloway."

"Thank you, *Señor* Otero. My men will take good care of the land that you have watched over for so many years. The range will not be overgrazed, I promise you."

She held out a quick hand. Otero took it graciously.

"I realize this is difficult for you, giving up your home place," she said gently, and hugged him, which almost brought him to tears.

"Furthermore," she said, seeing his pain, "we promise to share the apples with the bears."

Evan saw that she couldn't possibly have sealed the deal more kindly for the nearly overcome Benito, because he kept murmuring— *"Gracias, gracias, señorita."*—as the tears came. "My dear Amelia would be happy to know that."

"Now," she said, "you can go to *Señor* Keeley's tomorrow and sign over the deed and get your money. We'll notify him this afternoon about our agreement." She regarded him again, concern rising to her face. "Are you all right, now?"

He nodded, his lips forming a silent *gracias*.

"Then we can go," she said quietly.

Reading her thoughts, Evan sensed that she, too, shared part of Benito's sadness, realizing that Empire was taking something which he had long held dear and which he associated with the memory of his wife and children.

Kinder and Conklin were already on the way out.

She looked at Evan. He nodded and said: "You are very kind and generous. Thank you. It is hard for Benito, but he feels he must go."

"I can understand that. He had a good life here." She glanced at the open door. "I hope to ride out your way before long."

"I'll look for you."

Otero was weeping as she went out. "I have sold my

home," he lamented, turning to Evan.

Evan rested a comforting hand on the old man's shoulder. "I believe Miss Holloway will do what she promised about taking care of the ranch. It will be in good hands. It will be all right, Benito. You can feel good about that."

"Now I must pack up some things to take. A trunk or two. All memories." He almost broke down.

Evan held him, saying: "I understand there's a freight line out of El Paso going west through Rosita every few weeks that brings supplies to the store. Ask Keeley about sending your trunk. Get Pablo and Josefa to help you pack . . . you know they will."

"*Sí*. I must see about my money right away, Evan. How do you think I should carry eet? In a money belt?"

"No. What if the stage was robbed and you had all your money on you? Take what you think will be enough for food and lodging, then add a little more." He grinned at the old man. "Don't want you to get hungry. For the rest of your money, ask Keeley if he can make out a bank paper or bank draft that you can cash out there and deposit. Where are you going in California?"

"Los Angeles."

"Good. He must have connections there."

But he saw Benito looked discouraged and lost.

"Want me to go with you to see Keeley?"

"Please, *amigo* Evan."

"I will. Glad to."

"You are not too busy?"

Evan laughed. "I'm the biggest loafer in the valley."

"I am very tired. Will you stay a while now?"

"Of course."

"I have some tequila."

"You need a drink. I'll have some with water."

"There is nothing better than having tequila with a friend."

"I agree, Benito."

"We're just tryin' to save Empire some money when we hung up on the two dollars," Kinder said as they went to their horses.

"This little ranch is worth every cent I paid for it," Lucinda told him. "I believe it's a fair price, and I wanted to be fair to the old gentleman. We can call it our north pasture," she concluded with enthusiasm.

He started to give her a hand when she mounted, but she ignored him. She did not want the feel of his hand on her body. That must have flashed out in her face as she quickly swung to the saddle, because he took instant umbrage.

"Reckon it'd been just right to help you mount if I was that Captain Shelby?" he said curtly. "Him instead of me?"

His tone stung. "Nobody helps me mount, and you know it!"

She slapped the reins across Barney's withers and took off.

Kinder mounted fast and spurred up beside her. "No reason to get riled up," he said. "We need to talk."

"About what? Today's deal is done. You and Conklin couldn't have closed it the way you were headed . . . take it or leave it. Now, either you or Conklin tell Mister Keeley to make the money available at once for *Señor* Otero. There's nothing else to talk about today."

"There's plenty to talk about, Miss Cindy, if you'll listen. We're just gettin' started good, acquirin' pasture. Need to plan ahead. Need to talk this afternoon."

She realized she was being abrupt with him; after all, he was her foreman, she reminded herself, giving in. "You and Conklin come over after you see Keeley."

"Shore. We'll be there."

She had let him have his way, she thought, which wasn't good with Arch Kinder, who usually took more than granted and got away with it.

She rode to the livery, left her horse with her good friend Bear Webb, and walked slowly across to the hotel, feeling suddenly let-down. Hannah Young came out of the kitchen. She always greeted Lucinda with gladness; to Lucinda, it was the kind of welcome a girl would get from her mother when she came home after school—plain old happy anticipation and love.

"You look tired," Hannah said. "Better have some coffee."

"I'd like some. Thanks, Hannah."

"Are you just tired or troubled?"

She avoided Hannah's eyes by removing her hat, thinking she must hide her feelings better than this. Her father had taught her that there were matters you did not discuss even with warm friends—family matters, he'd meant. Arch Kinder was a family matter, a growing family problem that was not going away, instead, getting bigger and bigger. Flat menacing, instinct told her. It was about to get out of hand. She would have to stop it before it did. A decision she dreaded. But how?

She sipped the strong coffee, nodding, smiling contentment. "We bought *Señor* Otero's place today. He was so sad about selling, it made me sad about buying. Two dollars and seventy-five cents an acre."

"A good price these days," Hannah said. "It is good pasture."

"My people tried to hold him to two dollars. I knew that was too low. So I went up, and we shook hands on that."

"You're straight as a wagon tongue, Miss Lucinda. You

were brought up right."

"I wouldn't feel right cheating that sad old man."

Declining a second cup, she thanked Hannah and went up to her room, pulled off her boots with a bootjack, and stretched out on the bed, aware of the strung-out tightness of her body beginning to relax. Hannah and Hannah's coffee had helped. She thought how lucky she was to have found Hannah and her little hotel, a virtual refuge where she could rest and feel at ease and be herself and think for herself.

She must have drifted off to sleep, because the next thing she knew was a rap on the door. She got up, slipped into shoes, and went to the door.

When she opened it, Arch Kinder came in, alone.

Surprised, she asked: "Where's Conklin?"

"He decided to stay and drink with the crew for a while."

"You mean come over a little later?"

"He didn't say."

Kinder took off his hat and laid it on the small table by the window and sat down in the large chair there, an obvious sign to her that he intended to stay a while, instead of holding his hat and waiting to be invited to sit down.

An instinct, true and quick, informed her that his explanation of Conklin's absence was false.

"Did you tell Mister Keeley about buying *Señor* Otero's ranch, and the price?"

"We did."

"And he'll make the money available as soon as the deed is signed over to us?"

"We did."

Her senses picked up the smell of whisky, which she was used to at times around cowboys, and didn't mind, but she also caught the strong smell of bay rum, which she remembered cowboys had splashed on before going to dances. She had never smelled it on young men at chaperoned dances in St. Louis.

"Then I guess there's not much else to talk about today," she told him, an evident finality in her voice.

If he caught that, he didn't show it, insisting: "There's plenty to talk about."

"What do you mean?"

There was another chair on the other side of the table from him but she remained standing in the center of the room, a clear signal for him to cut short his visit, as clear as his conduct was to stay.

"We've bought up five thousand acres so far," he said, taking a little memorandum from his shirt pocket and glancing at it. "Most of it south of Rosita." He raised his gaze. "And for a damn' sight less than what you gave Otero today. You let that old Mexican's put-on act of feelin' sad get to you."

If Arch really wanted to talk business, that beat having to push him away, she decided, and took the chair opposite him.

"I don't agree," she countered. "It was a fair price for the range improvements that good. I don't think he was putting on. The old gentleman was hurting. Now he can leave and be with his folks and live out his days in peace."

"Me and Conklin have never paid more'n two dollars an acre, and most times less."

"You're both strong negotiators."

"Conklin is a great talker, as you know."

"With some intimidation thrown in, such as you both tried on *Señor* Otero."

"That was the same as walkin' away in a horse trade, figurin' the other man will call you back before you ride off."

"If you two had left, I don't think he would have called you back and sold for two dollars. He was just feeling sad and

99

wanted to be understood as a human being."

"Keep that up, Cindy, you might as well open a gospel tent."

"When Empire has ten thousand acres of good pasture in hand," she said flatly, "I think it will be time to call a halt before we do much more."

"Call a halt?" he echoed, startled. "Like I said, we're just gettin' started good. Why, we'll have ten thousand acres signed up in a few more weeks."

"I see it this way. Say five acres to a cow, ten thousand acres will support two thousand head. That's a good-sized spread this far from a shipping point. In Apache country, to boot."

"Don't believe Rip saw it that way."

"He wanted a good, working ranch out here. Nothing more. Not the biggest spread in the territory."

"You're forgettin' the markets not far away. The Army posts we can reach. The mining camps west of here. Silver and gold, then copper. Piños Altos is gonna be big, Keeley says. And there's more camps east of the Mimbres, on the other side of the Black Range, on toward the Río Grande. Army posts strung along the river as well."

"No doubt what you say is true, Arch, if a person wanted to control most of the best grazing land for the biggest spread . . . I don't. Neither do I think Father did. He was tired of fighting. It seemed to never end. He died fighting."

Kinder shook his head sadly. "He shore did. Must've fought to the last, knowin' Rip."

She and Kinder had discussed her father's death very little; it had been too difficult for her to bear at any length, and still was. In fact, she had hardly talked about it with anyone, even beloved Hap McCoy, other than learning the few facts of what had been found at the scene, then making wrenching arrangements for the funeral. Now Rip Holloway lay beside Lucinda's mother on a gentle wind-swept hill overlooking the ranch. From there he could observe his holdings forever, resting in the peace he never had.

"I doubt we'll ever know exactly what happened," she said.

"He must've been surprised somehow."

"Caught unawares? Hard to believe. He had the eyes of an eagle."

"There's a bushy rise there. I figure the *bandidos* happened to ride up on Rip when he was lookin' off at somethin' in the distance the other way. Still, he managed to get off a few shots before he went down. . . . Could be that was the way it was, Cindy."

"Now here we are in a beautiful valley in New Mexico, trying to carry out his dream. He was always so strong and alert. In my eyes he couldn't be brought down. He was not only my daddy, he was my hero."

Kinder looked down. "I know."

"I'm talking too much. And there's still much to be done." She knew she sounded tired; talking about her father had tired her even more. It was time for Arch to leave.

He reached across the table and took her hand. "You're a woman, and I'm a man. I don't mind fightin' for the brand or something I want. There's a once-'n-a-lifetime opportunity for Empire right here, all around us. Now is the time to grab it. I'd rather be the biggest spread any day than a pint-sized outfit held together with rawhide lookin' for favors. . . . This is your big chance, Cindy. Bigger even than Empire's Texas spread."

Your big chance, Arch, it ran through her mind, *Arch Kinder, the big* segundo *on horseback in New Mexico Territory.*

But because he was a man she couldn't blame him for entertaining such a vast dream, for his eagerness to seize what was out there. Except it was not her dream, and without her it wasn't possible. Withdrawing her hand, searching for the tactful words, she said: "Let's get the ten thousand acres first."

As he reached for her hand again, she stood up. She saw his face change swiftly at her refusal, his quickening of feeling. He got up and would not be denied when he took her arm.

"We can do this together, Cindy. Don't you see?"

Stepping away, she shook off his hand. But he reached for her again, pulled her to him with one sweep of his right arm and was going to kiss her on the lips, forcing her head back. But she turned her face away and took his hard kiss on her cheek bone as a wave of whisky and bay rum enveloped her.

"Arch! Stop it!" Instinct approaching panic moved her away from the bed at her back.

But he didn't stop while she stared at him in dismay and fear. He was not the obliging Arch Kinder of her father's time; she saw a wholly different person. He wore an expression she had never seen before—mouth set, eyes squeezed down, intent, burning. He was breathing fast. Then he grabbed her with both arms.

Fighting with both hands, she tore loose, whirled, and slapped his face with all her supple strength, the sound like a shot in the little room. The unexpected blow checked him, staggered him. His jaw fell. He rubbed his reddening cheek in disbelief. "By God," he muttered.

"Get out!" she said, raging, feelings hurt. "I'll have no more of this!"

He looked stunned.

"Don't ever come back here, unless I send for you. If I do, I'll make certain someone else is with me or you. I don't trust you any more." Her anger and hurt kept building the more she talked, and the full realization of what had nearly happened swept over her. A few more moments and. . . .

"I was just tryin' to make love to you," he said lamely.

"It was more than a hug or a kiss. Your idea of love is about like roping and tying and branding. You needed a rope. I should fire you. Get another person to run Empire."

That shook him out of his state of surprise. "You can't run Empire without Arch Kinder!"

"The hell I can't! I could run it myself if I had to. Father brought me up to work. I know cattle and horses. I can work with men. But I'd rather have a foreman I can trust . . . Hap McCoy would do fine."

He sneered. "That stove-up old cowpoke! He couldn't begin to handle it."

"Better say no more. You're on thin ice from now on. Now get out of here!"

He stood his ground.

"I mean it! Get out or I'll call for help." She did not expect him to apologize, and he did not surprise her by doing so. Expressing regret was not in him. Arch Kinder took what he wanted.

She marched to the door, opened it, and stood by, waiting impatiently. If he didn't leave, she would call for Hannah.

Kinder got his hat and departed without looking at her. His face was like stone as he passed her, his eyes like flint. Another ripple of fear smote her, left her shaking.

She closed the door and turned the key in the simple lock, then rested her back against the door in relief. Her mind was spinning as she found her way to the table and sat down. Suddenly she buried her face in her hands and let go, weeping, feeling alone, the worst moment of her life since the death of her father.

Hurry, Hap, I need you.

Chapter Eight

After a restless night, Lucinda Holloway was still shaken the next morning. At a breakfast of only coffee she had managed to avoid talking to Hannah, busy in the kitchen, aware that her keen-eyed friend might sense something amiss by the way she looked or said so little. Hannah had likely heard Lucinda raise her voice. As much as she liked and trusted dear Hannah, she would not discuss with her what had happened with Arch Kinder, or rather what had nearly happened to her. Again, it was family business. Ranch business. She knew she was going to fire Arch before long. She had to; if she did not, he would find her alone again, or, by some ruse, as yesterday. Next time it would take more than a hard slap to stop him; it would take a bullet. Meanwhile, with Conklin and that hardcase crew, he could continue to buy range until the Rip Holloway Ranch was assured.

Her mind trailed back. Arch Kinder owed Empire a great deal. Her father had taken him in as a young man, treated him almost like a son, although he didn't sleep in the house . . . after some years making him *segundo* on trail drives . . . as Arch himself had told her, saving him from the Owlhoot Trail. Her generous father, having no son, must have spoiled him along the way. Now Arch Kinder wanted too much and would take it if denied. She wondered why she had not noticed that trait before now. However, most times she had seen Arch with her father, at his side and doing his every bidding, or with others, and, when alone with her, only briefly. Never in a hotel room! She reasoned that her father's unexpected passing had left Arch with great expectations and an immediate assumption of absolute power, including over her.

It was nine o'clock when she crossed over to the livery. Bear Webb was coming back from the corral when she met him in the runway of the barn.

He halted in mid-stride. "Miss Holloway," he greeted her, always cheerful. "Goin' out this mornin'?"

"Not yet, anyway," she said, and glanced around, lowering her voice. "Bear, I need some particular help, and I thought of you first." She took another look around.

"Silas is on a little horse buyin' trip downriver. What can ol' Bear do for you? You know I will if I can."

"I want a gun."

"You have your Henry rifle. I keep it on your saddle. Cleaned and checked it out only yesterday."

"Thank you for that. I . . . mean I want a handgun."

He considered her curiously. "You needin' a handgun?" His tone told her that didn't sound quite seemly for a young woman like her.

Her smile failed to break through his doubt. "I don't mean a great big six-shooter. That would be awkward for me to handle, though I suppose I could with practice . . . if I wanted to strap on a gun belt and drink with the boys at the Gem."

He didn't see the humor of that, and remained questioning and puzzled.

"It just occurred to me I might need one sometime."

"Could be, but not likely for you, missy. Hope never. As for power, a big ol' six-shooter packs a heap more authority than a small handgun. And, generally, a man is in more dangerous places than a woman."

"I think," she said, frowning, "what I really have in mind is a Derringer. Could you get me one?"

At last he grinned at her, amused. "A little hide-out peashooter? Gamblers call 'em sleeve pistols. A card sharp

throws his arm out and snaps the pistol down into his hand."
He grinned again. "Least that's the way I saw it done the last
time I was in El Paso, which was a long time ago. . . . Now you
say you want one. I'll try to oblige you. Keeley keeps a reg'lar
arsenal at the store." He considered her again, serious and instructive. "Out ridin' you might need a rifle more than a six-
shooter, and a Derringer wouldn't be worth a whoop in hell."

"I don't want one for riding. I mean for on my person."

He pursed his torn lips, humoring her. But he still didn't
think her request made sense, and, in a changing voice of concern, he said: "You know, Miss Holloway, I wish you
wouldn't take them long rides without an escort. It worries
the heck outta me and Silas. It's plumb risky. An' I bet
Hannah worries, too."

His distress got to her. She reached out and touched his
arm. "I understand, and I thank you. I'm sorry I worried you
and Silas. I've only taken one long ride . . . that was downriver.
Last two times I crossed the river south of town and rode north
a little way, and each time I ran across Captain Shelby."

"That's better. Evan's a good man, Yankee or not. He
always stops by and visits."

"I promise I won't take another long ride by myself."

He gave her a huge, misshapen smile. "You make me feel
better. Now, I'll see what Keeley might have."

"I'd better give you some money."

"Not yet. Come back middle of the afternoon."

"Thank you, Bear."

She went to her room and rested, feeling relaxed, glad that
she exercised her right to defend herself if necessary. Her situation had taken such an unexpected turn. Never in her life
had she ever felt threatened until yesterday. It frightened her.
Her thoughts roamed back to her father and what had been
and to Hap McCoy—lulling thoughts.

It was afternoon when she opened her eyes. She had a late lunch and chatted a while with Hannah. Nothing was said about yesterday.

Bear Webb was waiting when she returned to the livery.

"Got a couple of little bangers for you to look at," he said, amused. "Surprised Keeley had even one. Kinda makes me wonder what he used to do 'fore he came to the valley. But that's not nice to say, is it?" He showed her a hook-handled little pistol, single barrel. "This is a Colt Derringer Number One. Forty-One caliber. That's a man-stoppin' slug. Take it. It's not loaded."

She took it gingerly, examined it.

"Here's another," he said. "A double-barreled Remington. A double man-stopper. Forty-One caliber. Two barrels, now. One atop the other."

She returned the Colt and took the Remington. "Which one do you like, Bear?"

"I don't like Derringers. It's up to you. How the gun feels in your hand."

"What is the range, Bear?"

"About fifteen feet. Not over twenty. A Forty-One slug that close would have the authority."

She thought it over, undecided.

"Let's go down past the corral near the river and fire 'em both. Then you'll know."

They walked down under a cottonwood. Webb slipped a cartridge in the single-barrel Derringer and handed it to her.

"There's no trigger guard," she said, frowning. "Where's the trigger?"

He smiled. "The trigger pops out when you cock the hammer. Now point toward the river, cock it, and fire."

She held it out, her movement uncertain. She cocked it

and pulled the trigger and blinked at the loud noise, the little gun kicking in her hand as powder smoke bloomed.

"Surprised you, didn't it?" he said. "Now try this double-barrel. It's single-action, like the first gun. You have to ear the hammer back for the second shot as you did the first."

She hefted it lightly and fired two deliberate shots, the barrels rotating as the gun recoiled. Handing it back, she said: "I believe I like the first gun better. Feels lighter in my hand."

"All right. I have a few shells." And, in a kindly, lecturing voice: "I hope you never have to use this little banger. If you do, it will mean you're in big trouble . . . your life is in danger. I shore hope that never happens, missy. But if it makes you feel safer to have it close, I'm glad you have it. Always shoot for the heart."

As they strolled back, he looked at her critically. "Just how will you hide or carry this little gun on your person?"

"You see, I have my purse. I could put it in that."

"Now, wouldn't that be just fine," he said, with heavy sarcasm. "Your purse is on the other side of the room, so you trip over there, open it, grab your dainty little Derringer, and stop the threat, which has to be a man. Meanwhile, he's had time. . . ." He waved off the thought. "I don't want to think about it. Let's take things in order. You won't need it riding. You have your rifle . . . but if you're inside somewhere and you feel a threat. You either have to have it on you, or close where you can grab it. Stick it inside a belt, or maybe a holster can be made for it." He frowned. "But you're supposed to hide a Derringer, not wear it in public . . . you want it to be a surprise." He shook his head. "Whatever you do, keep it on safety, so you won't shoot yourself with a Forty-One slug."

His concern made her feel guilty. "I'll be careful with it, Bear. I promise. How much is it?"

"Five dollars."

"Only five? I want to pay you for your trouble, too."

"No." He was emphatic, and she saw that he didn't like this at all as he handed her the three shells.

She paid him, slipped the Derringer and shells into her purse, hugged him hard, and left him shaking his head.

He wondered what was wrong. She was afraid of somebody. He couldn't think of any valley man. Her acquaintances were limited. It had to be somebody who'd come in from the outside . . . that meant in her own outfit. He stopped himself there and stood long in thought, watching her enter the hotel, conscious of an overwhelming wish to protect her. Not since he'd kissed his dear mother good bye at fourteen in Alabama, never to go back, to make his way out West, had he been so moved. Tears came to his eyes. Hell, he was old enough to be her father. She had no father. Rip Holloway was dead. Old Bear was still a man, despite the wreckage left by the grizzly. That damned Derringer worried him, a man who'd outfought the Apaches and made a living in the mountains, a man used to the blast of a big-caliber rifle.

As he turned back to his chores, it steadied in his mind that something was in the wind. Nothing had been the same since Empire rode into Rosita with riders who fit the mold of outlaws instead of cowboys. He'd keep his eyes open.

Chapter Nine

When she wasn't thinking of Hap McCoy, she was thinking of Evan Shelby. And there was a business letter to write to her bankers in El Paso. It was past ten o'clock when she mounted up. Saddling out of town at Barney's eager running walk, she noted the crew's horses lined up at the Gem, which also meant Arch and Conklin. A noisy place even at this hour.

The ten thousand acres played in her mind. When the outfit reached that goal, she would need Hap at her side when she broke the news to the riders that their work was finished. Go draw their pay. Also, Conklin for his glib services. And, last, all hell would break loose when she told Arch he was no longer foreman. She dreaded facing his explosive rage, but it had to be done.

Hap should be here before long, she reasoned. In her defenseless state, it would not be wise to take action without him. Whom could she call on if matters came to an early head? Mister Keeley? He struck her as a wise businessman who skirted trouble; yet, she would not blame him if he backed off from facing Arch Kinder. She didn't want to drag Evan into this mess. Nor Hannah, who would always provide moral support and a refuge.

What would her father advise in this situation if she were left to act on her own? She knew at once: *Do what you have to do, but be prepared to face the consequences.* In other words, she also knew, be ready to defend yourself. There was no easy way out.

She splashed into the Mimbres and halted midway, enjoying its unchanging chant, and rode on, heading for Evan Shelby's cabin. Once on the other side of the river, she always felt a vague release, a sense of peace.

She heard his—"Over here!"—before she located him beyond the cabin by the stream. Waving her on, he came out to meet her.

"Trying to lay a little stone walk from the slope down to the creek," he said. "I can't seem to find enough flat rocks nearby. I'll have to overlook my natural laziness and go looking. Step down and join me."

He led Barney off a short way and tied him to a juniper. Then he found a place for her on a fairly smooth rock facing the chirrupy little stream.

"This is nice," she said, removing her hat and brushing at her hair. "It's so peaceful, so restful, listening to your creek sing. It makes me wish I had the soul of a poet."

"Maybe you have, but have been too busy to put into use?"

"I wrote some poetry in school. My teacher urged me to do more."

"There you are, a budding poetess. Did you?"

"A little. I used to get homesick for the old ranch and write poems about Texas."

"That's good. Where did you attend school?"

She looked embarrassed. "Missus Pettigrew's School for Young Ladies in Saint Louis. My father's idea. Sounds so uppity. So snooty."

"Not at all. I recall hearing my mother say that some local girls were going there. I believe it has a good rating."

"Missus Pettigrew and her staff worked us hard, least we students thought so. My father was very pleased when I finished and brought home a diploma. Guess I really did it for him. He used to tell me how important a good education is. That the gun-toting times would pass, and so would the free range for the man who could take it and hold it, as he had done."

"Your father was right." He was curious. "Your mother had no voice in your schooling?"

"She passed on when I was small."

"I'm sorry . . . very sorry." He shook his head, pained for her. "I didn't mean to pry, though it must have sounded like it. Your father made certain your book learning was not neglected."

"You are relaxing to be around, Evan. You smile a lot. I enjoy talking to you. It's good to talk about something other than grass and water."

His smile widened. "As important as they are. It is thoughtful of you to ride out here. If I may say so, you are mighty good company, Miss Lucinda. I am honored. As for smiles, you make a man smile." Looking off, he missed her reaction. Turning back to her, he said: "I enjoy friendly people, and look forward once a week to riding into Rosita for mail and visiting a little. In order not to become too lazy, I give myself projects. This one will require a few more days."

"Can you reveal your next project?" she asked teasingly.

"Pleased to," he laughed. "Maybe that will spur me into action. After much deliberation, I've decided to build a porch so I can view the lower trail. As I say that, I realize I haven't finished my trail project . . . however, that is endless. Could go on for months."

She held her gaze on him for a considering moment. "Would I be prying if I asked about how long you plan to stay here?"

"Not at all," he assured her. "I really don't know." Which was both truth and evasion. He was skirting the question because this was not the right time to tell her, the moment laden with fear—that telling the truth might end their growing, cherished friendship.

To avoid more conversation in that direction, he excused himself and went to the cabin. Returning shortly, he handed her a thick little book.

"Yours," he said. "It's somewhat worn as you can see, but intact. Another survivor of the war."

"Lord Tennyson!" she exclaimed. "We studied him in school. Thank you, Evan. So much."

"You are most welcome. I don't like everything he wrote, but it helps to free the mind from the mundane demands of the day."

"I welcome it. I shall read it with new appreciation. Missus Pettigrew would be pleased. You are very generous. I realize your library must be limited here."

"Newspapers from back East provide plenty of reading. They're still hashing over the war back there, which tires me. Yet I know the effects will be with us for a long, long time. The deep South is hurting economically. Truth is, I am more interested in what's around me . . . all this pristine wonder . . . than much contemplative reading. Someday . . . I hope . . . a big part of this will become a protected national forest." He stopped suddenly, laughing at himself. "I am really lecturing, aren't I?"

"I am still listening, professor."

"I'll remember that when I make out the grades, Miss Holloway." She was making him smile now. "To cut this short . . . when I come in after working out . . . I feed my horse, cook supper, sit by the fireplace a while, reading some and nodding more, then hit the blankets. It's a lazy man's life." He would not tell her that he heard regularly from his mother, since she had lost hers a long time ago. And once again he thought of the hint of loneliness about her at times— first her mother, recently her father. More and more, he wanted to please her somehow, make her smile, laugh, if he could.

"After all this blow," he said, "would you listen to a lunch served in primitive, but, nevertheless, heartwarming, elegant, style by your obedient, almost cringing, servant?"

"Nothing would please me more, sir," she replied, holding the book close to her while assuming a lofty air, "provided it is done properly. That is the thing."

"Then come this way."

They were both into it now. As he made a show of escorting her to the cabin, she matched him by holding her head high and affecting a stately walk. When they neared the door, he swept the ground with his old hat and bowed at the entrance. By the time they entered, she was giggling.

"By the way," he asked, "did the celebrated Missus Pettigrew direct school plays for you young ladies?"

"Oh, yes. We all had parts. She had been on the stage in New York, also London, she said."

"She said?" Evan repeated, fixing her an oblique look. "You mean you questioned her veracity?" With another flourish, he showed her to a chair at the table.

"She was a stagey lady, and she always dressed like one coming on stage. When she entered the classroom, she was on stage again, and we were the audience. Yes, we all believed her. We dared not question her and try to pin her down for particulars."

"Did you budding thespians like her?"

"We respected her." She drew herself up. "I refuse to answer more questions about Missus Pettigrew, sir, on the grounds they might lead me into boggy footing."

"Request granted, Miss Holloway. If I have caused you even the slightest undue stress, delving into your impressive past, forgive me, please. But one more question, if I may, free of any dangerous bogs."

"Granted, sir."

"Did you feel like a lady after you finished school?"

"Hell, no!" she shot back. "Bartender, gimme a shot of red-eye!"

He roared with laughter and unfeigned astonishment.

"I shouldn't have said that," she quickly apologized. "I wanted to get back at you a little. The school was good for me. Missus Pettigrew was strict, and I needed that. I'd been spoiled. Most of all, it made Father happy. At the same time, I never forgot my people or where I was from. I'm proud to be a Texan."

He nodded to that. "One final question. While you were under Missus Pettigrew's tutelage, did you ever run away and come home?"

"I thought about it more than once my first year, when I got homesick."

"What if you had?"

"My father would have taken me right back. That's why I never did. He was determined to get me educated."

"I'd better see about some lunch," he said, turning to the stove, enjoying the good-humored bantering, thinking it was good for her. She was quick. He took out biscuits wrapped in a flour-sack cloth, the way his mother kept bread fresh at home. With his back turned, he busied himself cutting biscuits in half and heaping on preserves, making sandwiches.

"At last, the *pièce de résistance,*" he announced grandly, bringing a platter of the biscuits and placing a plate for her. He held the platter before her, and she took a biscuit.

"Maybe Marie Antoinette could have saved her head if she'd flung biscuits to the mob after she ran out of cake," he jested. "On the other hand, a bad batch might've riled 'em even more."

She nibbled. "Very good, Evan. You could hire on as trail cook." After a large bite: "Apricot preserves, aren't they?"

"Courtesy of the Garza family. Would you like some cold coffee?"

"Believe not. But I would like a glass of water."

He filled a glass from the cedar water bucket. It was from his glasses reserved for company, washed in hot soapy water, then rinsed in scalding water from the teakettle.

"When I first came here," he said, "I boiled every drop I drank from the little creek. I couldn't get out of my head the brackish, foul water we seemed to have at every bivouac the last year of the war. Men got sick . . . fever . . . coughing. We soon learned to boil it." He made a wry face. "Even strain it sometimes. But this water tasted so good, I decided to find out its source. On foot, I traced it to a little spring way up yonder. It's clean all the way down. Stock don't drink from it and break down the banks." He offered her an appeasing smile. "Not that I'm against ranching in the valley, *dear lady*."

She merely smiled and said: "I've had many a cool drink of water on a hot day, side by side with my saddle horse, both of us slurping it up. Never tasted better. There's something about the companionship a good horse gives you. A sort of sharing all that's around you."

He nodded again and again.

She held a teasing look on him. "Could you stand an old story I heard more than once growing up about what a good drink of water . . . or almost any water . . . means to an old cowhand on a hot day?"

"Go ahead," he urged her.

"I promise you it won't shock you."

She had him chuckling. "It would take a great deal to shock me, after being around horsemen so many years. Please

116

tell it, in detail. Don't hold back. I'll prepare myself, in case." He folded his arms.

"It was a very hot day," she began. "Slim and Shorty, these two ol' hands, had been up before daylight, workin' cattle. Not a drop of water all day. Hot wind blowin'. Late in the afternoon, they rode up on a little hole of water. . . . Slim got down, and Shorty rushed around to the other side. Men and horses started drinking.

"Pretty soon Slim, looking up, noticed that Shorty's horse was pawin' the water and had muddied it up considerable. Slim said . . . 'Why don't you come around over here, Shorty? My horse ain't muddied it up like yours.' "

She paused for effect.

"Don't keep me in suspense," Evan begged. "What did Shorty say?"

"Shorty, with his chin barely above the water, mumbled . . . 'It don't make a dang' bit of difference, Slim. I'm gonna drink it all anyway.' "

Evan let out a spontaneous laugh, then a chuckle.

"I hope that's not a forced laugh?" she said, eyeing him.

"A good story. And you told it with a drawling accent, instead of your Pettigrew manner of speaking."

He saw that he'd put it wrong without meaning to, because she said—"I hope you don't mean I sound stilted . . . just because I went away to school?"—and looked hurt.

"Oh, no! I didn't mean that. You don't at all. You just speak well, as an educated person, which is fine. Yet, you have retained the soft accents of a young lady brought up in Southwest Texas. I wouldn't change you one bit. I like hearing your voice."

She flushed at his frankness. To cover her momentary confusion and his own, he held out the platter of biscuits, and she took one. He had spoken without thinking, from the heart. It surprised him now, but he was glad that he had.

After a pause, keeping his voice careful, he said: "I want to ask a personal question that comes to my mind, hoping it doesn't make you sad. Do you . . . resemble your dear mother?"

"Father used to say so . . . very much . . . and I was so glad."

"Good. Now I know that she was very lovely."

She blushed and looked off. "It is sweet of you to say that."

Silence enveloped them. Again, he had spoken on impulse.

Then, in a thoughtful way, he said: "I've been thinking about another ride we might take before long, if you're not too busy. Farther than our jaunt to the votive spring. It's a ride to Emory Pass, to the top of the mountains. They say it's quite a view from there. Think you might like that?"

"Oh, yes!"

"I'll look into it some more, report soon. There's a trail."

"All right."

"It might take most of the day, but back before dark."

"That would be all right."

"We'd need to take a lunch. More than my bachelor biscuits."

"I'll ask Hannah to pack us a lunch. I'll do that."

"Whatever you'd like," he said, thanking her. Seeing his Spencer against the wall, he pursed his lips. "It's always a good idea to plan ahead, since we'll be on a long ride. You'll have your Henry rifle. Fifteen shots in the magazine."

"And one in the chamber," she said. "I wouldn't pack a rifle not fully loaded."

"You were brought up right."

"It was a gift from my father when I graduated. Its range is up to a thousand yards. I went deer hunting a few times and used it at target practice and shooting at coyotes and wolves during calving season. It's easy to handle and accurate, but awkward to load. The magazine is under the barrel, and you poke the shells in at the muzzle end. Wouldn't do to try that on the run, would it?" She laughed.

"But with sixteen shots a rider wouldn't have to reload very often. Sure beats the rate of fire of a single-shot muzzleloader. Your father was wise. I'm glad you have it and know how to use it."

His approval pleased her; he saw that in her eyes. Then she put a silencing forefinger to her lips. "Here I am telling you all about a Henry, and you've known about it for years."

"I knew of the rifle in the war, but Henrys were not issued. A few officers bought them. In the cavalry we had Springfield carbines, and in 'Sixty-Three the Spencers, like the one you see over there against the wall."

"I'm really not fond of guns. To me, they're just something you need around a ranch. But tell me about your Spencer. It has a very short barrel."

"Because," he grinned, "it's a carbine. Holds seven cartridges in the magazine, loaded in the butt stock. The magazine has a spring that pushes the cartridges forward after one is fired. With another one in the chamber, it's an eight-shooter. The hammer is pulled back for each shot. Its range is under your Henry by about five hundred yards or so. It packs a wallop . . . Fifty-Two caliber. A cartridge box called the Blakeslee Quickloader came into use late. It contains tubes of seven cartridges each. You remove the empty magazine, tilt the tube, and slide the cartridges into the butt stock, reinsert the spring-loaded magazine, snap it shut, and the gun is ready. I had no wish to bring a Quickloader out here. Just the carbine, because it's a familiar weapon, if needed, and a Colt

Army Forty-Four. I always carry a few extra cartridges."

"So do I."

"Which I hope you never need." He had been speaking in an instructive tone about the weapons. Now he looked at her with a gentle teasing. "As expected, you got a deer your first time out with the Henry?"

She hid her face with both hands. "I got buck fever. The rifle kept wobbling in my hands. I shot . . . must've missed by a mile, and the deer vanished. Father laughed at me . . . that made me mad. Eventually I got one. After that, I left the hunting to Father, who enjoyed it."

They chatted on, and the afternoon seemed to slip away on flying feet. At times he sensed that she desired to know more about him, why he had come West, but, beyond the early question as to how long he planned to stay here, she was too well-mannered to pry further, and he filled in no gaps.

When she thanked him for the book and the lunch and made ready to go, he made light of the meal's simplicity and, going out with her, brought her horse to the cabin. As she securely placed the book in a saddlebag and turned to Evan, a silence fell between them.

"I enjoyed the visit," she said.

"So did I. Very much. You are kind to ride out this far."

"Not kind, Evan. I wanted to come." A downcast look rose to her face, therein an elusive wistfulness. Her voice seemed to grow small and uncertain. "I'll be glad when I get the ranch established and I can honestly say I have fulfilled my father's wishes."

"You will. It takes time. This is quite an undertaking."

"We are acquiring land, but. . . ."

He wondered if more than land was distressing her. But she was young, and the young were always impatient. Yet, why not be?

"The sun comes up every morning, Lucinda. Before very long you'll have your ranch. I know you will."

She fastened suddenly shining eyes on him. "You always make me feel better, Evan . . . and happy."

He hardly knew what to say, if anything. Sometimes it was better to say nothing; and he deliberately put his arms around her and held her close, aware of her slim, young body fully against him. And feeling he could not, must not, kiss her on the lips, as much as he longed to, he kissed her on the cheek and released her and stood back, smiling his encouragement.

The heavy and meaningful silence grew between them again. He said: "Let me know if you need me for any reason. I'll come."

In another moment he feared she was going to cry. But she didn't. She seemed to take an inner grip on herself, murmured—"Thank you, Evan."—swung lightly to the saddle, and reined away, looking back at him as she rode off.

He would have to tell her before long. This could not go on day after day, based on what he knew within himself and what he thought he possibly but not absolutely sensed in her—yet not a word spoken between them. His continued silence about himself was unfair to her. He knew that she must wonder about him. Why would a former Union officer come to the Gila Wilderness and live alone in a cabin and do nothing? No semblance of endeavor. Not an artist, not a poet, not a naturalist. Nothing. Which left open any number of wild guesses. He might be a criminal for all she knew.

His eyes never left her. As he hoped, and as before, she reined about and waved when she came to where the trail made a descending bend. She appeared to linger as she looked back, still waving. He was still waving when she dropped out of sight.

She had wanted to stay longer. But best not. In another

minute, she might have let go and told him her fear of Arch Kinder, and other feelings, which had no place now with ranch problems. Again, she wondered about Evan. Why was he here? She had asked him how long he planned to be here, which really was prying, and he had avoided a direct answer; perhaps he didn't know. But why? She had yet to ask Hannah about him—that would be prying! But the way her feelings were running, she felt she must know more.

Her thoughts were heavy as she rode toward the river, thinking of the decision that awaited her regarding Arch Kinder. She refused to burden Evan with it, although she knew he would stand by her side if she asked. The decision might come before Hap arrived; if so, she must face it alone, as her father would expect her to as Rip Holloway's daughter.

Lost in thought, she suddenly sensed that the horseman in the woods across the river must have been watching her for some time before she sighted him, even when she was waving at Evan. She halted at once.

At that, the horseman flashed out of sight. He was riding a bay horse. She had only a glimpse of the rider—that was all. She didn't recognize him. But he had to be the same rider she had seen watching her previously. Was it Arch Kinder? She was tempted to send a shot from the Henry high into the timber where the fleeing rider might be, but dismissed the impulse as too reckless.

Cold fear gripped her. With a wrench, she thought of riding back to Evan—but that wouldn't do. She must settle herself. After a short while, she rode on, at the same time drawing the Henry and earing back the hammer for a shot. Reaching the river, she scanned the trees for a searching interval. The rider had vanished. She then tried to attribute it to happenstance; common sense informed her otherwise. Once, maybe. Not twice.

She reseated the Henry in its saddle boot, let Barney have his drink, and, making for the road, she found the trampled place from where the rider had watched. The numerous horse tracks told her that he had waited a long time.

Jogging into town past the Gem, she saw the full hitching rack mostly with bay horses. From where the rider had watched her, to here, wasn't far enough to make a horse break sweat.

She rode on to the livery. Bear Webb was in the last stall, examining the left foreleg of a saddle horse. He had not been in position to notice who passed on the street.

"This saddler has been packin' too much weight," Bear told her. "Silas just bought 'im, then found out he's a little lame. I'm gonna recommend we take off his shoes and turn 'im out in a sandy pasture by the river for a while."

"Makes sense to me," she said.

"What we need around here is a good vet."

"I think you're doing pretty well."

"Sympathy can go just so far, Miss Holloway."

He took her reins, and she walked across to the hotel with the book. Hannah was in her office. She waved.

"By chance have you noticed a man on a bay horse come in on the south road the last few minutes?" Lucinda asked her.

"No. I've been in the kitchen. Just came in here. Something wrong?"

"Oh, nothing, I guess. I've been out to Evan Shelby's since this morning. A while ago, coming back, I saw a man on a bay horse watching me from the timber on the south side of the river. When I noticed him and pulled up, he rode off fast. I waited a bit before I crossed the river. By the time I reached the road, there was nobody in sight."

"Probably somebody just ridin' by happened to be lookin' your way when you happened to look up and see him," Hannah said, shrugging.

"I would like to believe that, Hannah, but it's the second time it's happened. If he wasn't watching me, why did he ride off so fast?"

Hannah took that in without a change of expression, evidently trying to make little of it. "If it happens again, it might be something to worry about."

"If it does, I intend to fire a warning shot."

"Has it always happened coming back from Captain Shelby's?"

"Yes. Always."

"*Hm-m-m.* Did you have a good time?"

"Yes, I did. He gave me a book of poetry. We had lunch. Then we talked and talked about many things, and laughed a lot. He never talks about himself or the war. He's a very nice man. Very kind."

Hannah seemed to hesitate before she said: "I'm glad you had a good time. I believe you're even blushing a little."

A flood of warm feeling rushed over Lucinda. With a somewhat hurried—"Thanks for listening."—she left the room. She was going upstairs, when the impression registered that Hannah had been on the brink of saying more, then had thought better of it.

I guess my good time showed, she thought, and didn't mind. As for the rider on the bay horse, she had lived in danger-plagued Southwest Texas too long to ignore an apparent threat. Next time she would fire a warning shot. Meanwhile, she must be more alert, always looking around as she rode, as her father had taught her, and as Bear Webb had cautioned.

Chapter Ten

It was late afternoon, and the Gem, as most times, was crowded with Empire's noisy riders. Whisky was dirt cheap at fifteen cents a shot, despite the high freight charge from as far as El Paso by way of Las Cruces. Too cheap, in the opinion of Cap Shaw behind the bar. To cut down the brawls and the attendant rough stuff, he had suggested upping the price to two bits, but Keeley had said no, saying he feared trouble if he did. Someday, Shaw reckoned, William J. Keeley would be one of the richest men in the territory, if he wasn't already.

To Shaw, a saloon should be more like a club, where a man could drop in for a drink, chin a little, get in on the news, if any, and go on. Like Dave Logan. Good man, Dave. If plenty of time, play poker. The Gem had been like that, a quiet oasis, until Empire's arrival. The well-paid bunch even brawled among themselves. A former Texan who'd played on the rough side himself in his wild, younger days, Shaw could spot a hardcase at a glance. There was a swagger to most of 'em, and they all wore their guns tied down for a fast draw. He wondered how many were on the *cuidado* from the Texas Rangers or elsewhere. How many went by their real names? How many had been gone long enough to use their real names? He'd bet a good half of 'em went by Tex alone. Now and then, to keep peace along the bar, he would throw in a noncommittal—"Ain't it the truth?" or "So they say."—and grunt a laugh at their smutty jokes. If matters ever got out of hand with the Empire boys, he kept a .45 under the bar, ready for business. He would not kowtow or take insults to avoid

125

trouble. He had left the Lone Star State a free man, looking for more peaceful climes, as the poet might say, and so he would remain, true to himself.

He'd not read many books but he had a memory for "good sayin's," as he called them, and occasionally an Empire hand would ask his opinion on various matters, and Shaw would oblige. Shaw guessed he had that status because they knew he was Texas-born, and, being older and lean and grizzled with a proud handlebar mustache, he must know something. If a rider was in the process of breaking a new mount and bragging about being a bronc' stomper, Shaw might say: "Remember, boys, there ain't no hoss that can't be rode. At the same time, there ain't no rider that can't be throwed. Works both ways."

He might act as a peacemaker with: "Sometimes, boys, it's safer to pull your freight than to pull your gun." Or: "One thing for certain, boys, takin' another man's life shore don't make no soft pillow at night while on the dodge, lookin' up at the stars." If a rider came out on the short end of a horse trade, he might put his hand on the loser's shoulder and say: "Remember, man's the only animal that can be skinned more'n once, an' it happens to all of us, sooner or later." Sometimes, seeing the Empire riders wobbling out the swinging doors on high-heeled boots, Cap Shaw thought, *a man might think walkin' was a lost art.*

Now, glancing around the long, narrow room, he saw Arch Kinder and Code Sloan in earnest conversation at a table. Kinder struck Shaw as an ideal foreman for this short-trigger bunch. An impressive-looking man—big, full-chested, aggressive. Bold eyes that swept the room. An overbearing, overpowering, dominant man. A stallion of a man among lesser beings. The eyes went with his physical side, in them a driving, ruthless quality that said he would brook no interference in his path. His voice fit as well—strong, direct, compelling, impatient. As a saloonkeeper would, Shaw had observed that, although Kinder drank, he did not get drunk. He was always in restraint.

Code Sloan was a different shade—tough, reckless, cruel, a bully with cat-like quickness, headed for hell where a cooler man would send him someday. It would be interesting to know how many graves he had actually filled. Drinking, he bragged how tough he'd been in Texas. How many men he'd shot, not counting Mexicans and Indians. Discounting part of that as hot air, Cap Shaw still figured Sloan was by far the main gunslick in the outfit.

"I've got a special job for you, Code," Kinder was saying while he toyed with his untouched glass of whisky. "Might say it's a favor."

Sloan was only remotely interested. He'd been drinking all afternoon. By sundown he'd be drunk. "What is it?" he drawled.

"Empire has a big problem. A certain individual is holding up our plans to acquire enough range for Miss Holloway's ranch. You know what that means? It defeats our very purpose for being here." Kinder knew it wasn't true, but Code Sloan didn't. *Make it sound important*, Kinder told himself. *Affects the whole outfit. As a matter of fact, Lucinda Holloway's ten thousand acres weren't far away.*

"You mean . . . ?" Sloan asked, leaving it hanging, yet knowing.

"I want it done in a certain way."

"Why not make it simple? Bushwhack 'im?"

"No. This has to be done as a face-off. Here in the saloon, when he comes in for a drink. Work up to it. Something is said. Make it sound like an insult to you. It's got to look good."

"Who is this *hombre*?"

"Evan Shelby. Ex-Union captain. The man whose Spencer carbine you wanted that day in front of the store."

"Yeah. I almost had me a Spencer."

"What do you say, Code?"

Sloan flung Kinder his disgust. "Hold on! I risk my neck, but you make it sound easy. Shelby may be fast . . . you don't know. Never know what might happen against a stranger. I ain't no fool."

"You can take him. He's no hand with a six-gun."

"Bushwhackin's easy and sure."

"You miss the point. This has got to look respectable. A quarrel in the Gem. Hot words lead to a gunfight."

"What's in it for me?"

"Five hundred cash. I'll get it out of the ranch fund."

Sloan still balked. "You make it sound easy, but a face-off is always risky."

"Not afraid, are you?"

"There's a difference between bein' afraid and not bein' a fool. I ain't no fool, Arch. It's my hide. I'd have to think about this."

Kinder brought the full force of himself to bear on Sloan—his flinty stare, his voice, his physical appearance. "Believe your memory's slippin' bad, Code. You're forgettin' the time I went your bail in DeWitt County when you shot that deputy, and you skipped out to old Mexico. Cost me a thousand dollars."

"An' if I hadn't jumped bail, they'd hung me for certain."

"And still would, if your whereabouts was known."

"You mean, if I was back in DeWitt, hidin' out in the buck brush?"

"Don't matter where you are. You see, Code, I happen to know your name is now in the Texas Rangers' crime book, which lists the names and descriptions in detail of all wanted men. There's a sizable reward out for Code Sloan . . . two thousand dollars." Kinder didn't know whether Code Sloan was in the crime book or not, or about a reward, although he could well be. But pour it on. Throw fear into him. Rangers were the greatest fear a killer could have.

Sloan sat back, startled and concerned. His pinched features had turned pale. "Rangers' crime book? How'd you hear that?"

"Out of El Paso. Empire has connections there. You know that."

"Just what does this mean?"

"It means that, if the Rangers got wind that Code Sloan was here, they'd send a man to Rosita soon as they could get 'im on a stage with an arrest warrant. Bring Sloan in for trial. If you can't take Sloan alive, kill 'im. Rangers will go anywhere in the country for a fugitive . . . New York or California. They still think you're in old Mexico. They don't know you slipped into Arizona a few years ago, rode for cow outfits under another name, and laid low."

"Just shot Mexicans and Indians."

"You're braggin'. The only smart thing you've done was to stay in touch with me. The friend who went your bail and saved you from a sure hang rope. Probably the only true friend you've ever had. A friend you don't deserve after what's on your record or if you refuse to return a favor." Kinder was being blunt, laying it on heavy. When Sloan evaded his eyes, Kinder drove his voice at him. "Listen to me! You gonna do this or not? If you fail me, Code, don't be surprised if a ranger steps off the stage from El Paso with that warrant."

Sloan's mouth sagged. "You wouldn't turn me in, would you, Arch?" He was begging, just where Kinder wanted him.

"Don't want to. Would hate to do it."

Sloan's thin voice broke even higher. "Me, an old friend? We go back a long ways, Arch. Them slick deals on the side, cuttin' stock off the main herd, that old Rip Holloway never got wind of. If he had, you'd be pushing up Texas sod right now. If I spilled a few words to Miss Holloway, you'd be out on your thievin' ass . . . Arch Kinder, the trail *segundo* and trusted ranch foreman. That girl's got spunk."

"If you're fool enough to pull that, all I'd have to do was say Code Sloan was afraid I'd turn him in to the rangers for murder . . . which I'd damn' shore do. Meanwhile, have you held here in custody till the ranger arrived to take you back for hangin'. And," he gloated, "put in for the reward."

Sloan's gaze dropped. He was weakening, just as Kinder knew he would. Code Sloan was a coward. Then, doggedly, Sloan said: "Five hundred ain't much for killin' a man, Arch. You'll have to raise the ante. I'll do it for seven hundred."

Kinder laughed so uproariously he drew eyes. "If you ever saw five hundred at one time, it was when you robbed a stage. Five hundred it is. No more."

"That case, I'd have to have it in advance."

"Like hell! I know you, Code. You'd get drunk and blow it 'fore you did it, even blab about it. You can't keep your mouth shut. I'll give you a hundred now . . . the rest when you do the job. Meanwhile, there's another deal I can throw your way before long. Damn' good money. Big money . . . for you and a few of the boys. Over a thousand dollars."

"What is it?" Sloan asked eagerly.

"Later. I'll tell you later, soon as I see how it shapes up."

From his wallet, held under the table, Kinder took several greenbacks. Sloan accepted them without argument, just as Kinder knew he would.

"When does this Yank come in here?" Sloan asked.

"Every Friday, about mid-morning or so, for mail and supplies."

"Does he always come in here for a drink?"

"Don't know. May not. That's up to you to work out. You sit outside and wait. Act mad."

Sloan took that in, sorting things out, and said: "I can say he's been mouthin' around town I tried to steal his carbine, when all I wanted to do was look at it."

"Sounds good."

Kinder held up his right hand for Cap Shaw to see and pointed to Sloan. Shaw nodded, poured a shot of whisky, and served it. Shaw knew to put it on Kinder's bar bill.

"It's a deal, then," Kinder said after Shaw left.

Sloan had perked up, saying—"You know you can depend on me, same as you did in them border cattle deals."—and reached for the whisky.

Chapter Eleven

The westbound stage, painted in floral designs of red, gold, and yellow on the door panels, waited in front of Keeley's store, six fresh mules dancing nervously in the traces. Friends had gathered to bid Benito Otero good bye, a somewhat downcast crowd, because friendly, generous Benito, always a good neighbor and church-going man, had lived in the valley most of his life. It was sad to think they probably would not see him again. They spoke in soft voices, reminiscing about Benito and his family and what he had done for others. At this time he was in the Gem having drinks with Pablo Garza and other friends. For a leave-taking, it seemed rather quiet.

A whisky drummer from Kansas City, order book in hand, stood in front of the store having last words with Keeley. The drummer was a passenger with a young second lieutenant returning from leave back East to his post at Fort Bayard, and a burly miner in rough clothing who kept talking about reports of a gold and silver strike at Piños Altos.

The crowd knew it was time to go when Pete Dyer, the veteran stage driver, left the saloon and spoke to Keeley. Then he called out: "Time to git along. All aboard!"

Al Lane, the veteran shotgun guard, his usual reckless manner even more evident after a couple of drinks, came out at the sound of Dyer's voice and, showing the crowd a loose grin, followed Dyer to the stage.

Now Otero and Garza and two others emerged. Seeing the assembly of friends, Otero paused and came close to breaking into tears. But he forced a great smile of appreciation and

132

went slowly on, each step reluctant. He wore a dark suit and brown shirt with a blue scarf at his throat that had been Amelia's. Instead of a big sombrero, today he favored a small gray hat with a short brim. His Sunday boots glistened.

As he continued toward the stage, men held out their hands, and he grasped each one in his strong, work-hardened grip, and women touched him, and now and then a tear ran down an upturned face.

A woman's choked-up voice broke the silence. "We love you, Benito." Others joined in.

"We won't forget you, Benito."

"You must stay with us when you come back, Benito."

"Send us your address, Benito."

"God bless you, dear Benito."

The voices tore at his heart. By the time he reached the stage, he was near collapse, in acute mental and physical pain. Never once had he understood that leaving would be so difficult, almost impossible for a man to bear.

Garza took Otero's one piece of baggage from a wagon and placed it in the leather-covered rear boot of the stage, then turned in parting to Otero. They faced each other for a hurting, final moment, mouths crimped. Suddenly Garza gave him an *abrazo* with both arms, feeling his old friend's tension. That, and Garza patted him on the shoulder and went slowly back to Josefa, who was holding a handkerchief to her face.

Now Otero faced the crowd. His eyes traveled over them, back and forth, as if touching each one in fond remembrance. Another lingering look and, with a little wave, he entered the stage, and those gathered saw Benito Otero no more.

There was a stir as the whisky drummer, a red-faced man of generous physical proportions, passed through the thinning crowd to the stage. It sagged as he took the step and pulled himself through the narrow doorway with both arms, a gold watch chain across the vest over his melon-shaped paunch stretched to its length.

Dyer, known as a careful driver, walked down one flank of the mule teams, then the other, inspecting the hookups. Once he peered hard at a bridle, and moved on, that was all.

Bear Webb, watching from the livery, smiled to himself. Pete Dyer had yet to find anything amiss with the way Bear harnessed teams. If he ever did, Bear would never hear the last of it.

As Dyer climbed to the box, Bear noticed that he put nothing in the small compartment under the seat. No strongbox this time. Lane took position at Dyer's left as guard. He packed two six-guns and a shotgun loaded with buckshot. Lane had shot it out more than once, the story ran, with stage robbers and Apaches.

Dyer, a bit out of sorts when he saw his other two passengers hadn't loaded, faced the saloon and called out: "This stage is leavin'!"

At his words the miner and the second lieutenant hurried out, the miner waving a bottle of whisky. The officer, a boyish-looking young man, seemed embarrassed by his drinking companion's conduct. They made haste, the lieutenant the first to make the stage. The sturdy miner propelled himself inside with one thick arm.

Dyer sent one last look around, shook the reins, yelled at his tough hybrids, and the stage surged forward with a chatter of rattles and snapping leather.

A sad face appeared hauntingly at a window, then vanished. It was Benito Otero. Too late to wave, but everybody did.

"Is he doing the right thing?" Josefa asked Pablo.

"He is doing what is in his heart."

"Why couldn't he bring his people to live with him here?"

"They like California."

"Too bad. It is better here."

The passengers settled down, Otero next to the whisky drummer, facing forward. The lieutenant seemed to be enjoying himself as he idly observed the passing scenery. The miner crossed his arms and leaned back, cuddling his corked bottle. The narrow road was sandy as it followed the curve of the Mimbres, and the heavy stage rocked gently on leather thoroughbraces. Now and then the river gleamed through the timber and brush like splashes of silver. Otero followed it with fixed eyes, his mind reaching back to what he had left forever, home place and friends. As he had countless times, he lectured himself that he was doing the right thing. It was also his duty. Family was everything.

The miner uncorked the bottle and genially announced: "Anybody like a drink of extra good whisky?" He looked first at Otero, who declined with a shake of his head.

He then regarded the drummer, who let the suggestion of a smile play across his face before he said: "May I ask what brand that is, sir? Your hand covers the label."

"Old Green River," the miner proclaimed, tapping the bottle. "My favorite."

"I must compliment you on being a judge of good whisky. I happen to sell Old Green River, with a few other brands."

"Well, I'll be damned! Then you'd better have a drink with me."

"Thank you, sir, but I don't drink."

"What?" The miner shot him an incredulous stare that bordered on rank pity.

"My vice is food, which you can tell by looking at me."

Shaking his head, the miner offered the bottle to the lieutenant, who took a stiff drink without change of expression, expressed his proper thanks, handed back the bottle, and returned to observing the countryside.

"I'll say this . . . ah, Captain," the miner said admiringly, "you hold your whisky like a man."

"I'm a second lieutenant," the young man grinned. "What you mean is, I don't show it."

"You sure don't."

"There's a knack to it. You train yourself. Sometimes it's not easy. This is good whisky."

Pleased, the miner had a drink and sat back.

They were rushing along, the tireless mules taking to the sandy footing, a breeze off the river at their backs. Otero sat like a stone image, struggling in vain to shut out thoughts of all he had left forever. And then a saving glimmer broke through the fog in his tortured mind, like a prayer answered— he would return every year to Amelia's grave, and he would place fresh flowers on her grave, and he would plant many flowers there, and he would make certain it was clean of weeds, and he would stay with Pablo and Josefa, and they would invite friends in, and they would drink tequila, and they. . . .

Dyer's shrill yell of warning cut through his joyful musings of deliverance and threw him instantly alert. Glancing out the window, he saw brush piled high across the narrow road, blocking it. Dyer was raging as he fought to slow the teams. As the stage swayed and Otero grabbed the tug strap by the window, he could hear Dyer's foot brake squealing.

Everything was happening fast before Otero's eyes. Dyer slowed the mules down, under control, but not until they got into the brush. Now they were lunging and frantic, while Dyer fought to back them out of the tangle. At the same moment four masked riders dashed out of the river timber, six-shooters ready, shouting: "Hands up! Hands up!"

Al Lane put a barrel of buckshot into the lead rider, who grabbed his chest and pulled away. The others shot at Lane. Otero, peering out, glimpsed Lane slumping sideways.

Suddenly the shooting ceased. Dyer had the teams backing up, still frantic, still plunging, but under tight rein.

"Everybody out on this side!" One bandit, riding back and forth on a bay horse, was running the hold-up. Two others covered the stage. The man Lane had shot was halted in obvious pain at the edge of the timber.

When Dyer didn't obey the command, the rider shouted at him: "I said git down here, by God!"

"Do . . . an' these mules will take off like scalded cats!" Dyer shouted back.

"Then hand down your gun."

Dyer pitched his six-shooter down.

"Don't git smart. Now, the guard's guns. God dammit, move!"

Dyer carefully set the safety on each weapon and dropped them down with care.

"Now, everybody out!"

Otero got out first, followed by the lieutenant and the miner, still clutching the bottle. The drummer materialized slowly, like a bear emerging from hibernation.

The boss bandit dismounted and handed the reins to another.

"Drop your guns and stand in line. Hands up. Don't make any god-damned moves!" His voice was high, and Otero, worried that he might kill one of them in his nervousness, formed a ragged line with the other passengers.

Otero had no gun. Neither did the others.

The bandit didn't believe what he saw. "Where are your guns?"

Otero shrugged.

"I am not armed," the lieutenant said.

"No hide-out gun?"

"No gun. You have my word."

"A Yankee's word?"

"That's right."

The bandit sneered. The lieutenant said no more, but his eyes spoke for him.

"If you'd had a gun, soldier boy, reckon you'd used it when we stopped the stage?"

"*Reckon* I would have."

"Why ain't you packin' a gun?"

"I'll be issued weapons when I reach Fort Bayard."

"Figger you'll git there, do yuh, soldier boy?"

"*Figger* I will."

The bandit caught the repeated emphasis on words and stiffened. He was drawing back when a rider, sounding like an older man, broke in: "You're wastin' time. Line 'em up!"

The bandit stopped, jerked around, nodded. "Yeah. Line up! Throw your wallets on the ground!"

Four wallets flopped in the sandy soil. The bandit glared up at the driver. "You too, *hombre!*" And the driver obliged.

Coming to the drummer, the bandit started to take the gold watch chain. The drummer put out an imploring hand. "My wife gave me that on my last birthday. Appreciate if you'd not take it. There's a hundred dollars in my wallet."

The bandit's response was to jerk free the chain and watch and jam everything into a pocket, then clean out the wallet.

At the renewed urging of the hurry-up rider, the bandit rifled through the lieutenant's rather thin wallet, and then the driver's, also lean. From the miner's he took bills and a couple of gold coins. Just now discovering the precious bottle of Old Green River, he said: "Gimme that."

The miner said nothing, still clutching the bottle.

"God dammit, I said, gimme that!" the bandit shouted, making clear his intent to pistol-whip the miner if he refused.

"Come on! You're wastin' time!" the older bandit broke in.

"I want that whisky. Gimme that!"

The miner didn't budge.

The bandit slammed him across the head with his pistol barrel. Blood flew. Still, the miner held on. When Otero and the lieutenant moved to aid the miner, the bandit held them off with a six-gun.

It was like that for a suspended moment as the action stopped, a tableau, as if they were all actors on stage frozen in position, until the miner coughed out—"Take it. No whisky's worth dyin' for."—and gave up the bottle.

The bandit grabbed it, and Otero and the lieutenant stood back. While giving orders and constantly turning his head, the bandit's red bandanna had slipped. A curtain might have parted as Otero saw, full-on, a face he'd seen around the store and the Gem. A pinched face with a taut mouth and grayish beard and jumpy, pale eyes. Hastily the bandit pulled the bandanna over his nose.

In dread, Otero saw that it was his turn now.

The bandit emptied Otero's wallet of its few greenbacks, then glared at him. "Only fifty bucks! Don't hold out on me, you slippery Mex! Where's that big pay-off money?"

"Pay-off?"

"You just sold your ranch. You're leavin' for California. Where's the money?"

"Still at Keeley's."

"Like hell! You wouldn't leave without it. Empty your pockets."

Otero showed some change and a pocket knife.

"Hold your coat open."

The inside coat pocket produced a pencil, a letter, and Otero's eyeglasses, which the bandit threw down and ground under his boot. Otero flinched, but did not protest.

"Come on! Time to go!" the older rider prodded.

With a headshake of disgust, the bandit stepped to his horse and mounted. In a flick of time they were gone, dashing toward the river, the wounded rider spurring to keep up.

As they rode deeper into the timber, a rider complained: "Hell, Code! I thought you said that old Mexican would have the money on him?"

"Arch said he would. He sold his ranch."

"Not much to show for Jess gittin' shot an' us shootin' the guard."

"Not gittin' softhearted, are you, Murdo?"

"If I was, I wouldn't be where I am right now."

Otero, still warily watching, didn't ease down until the riders were out of sight, thankful Josefa Garza had sewn the bank draft inside the lining of his coat. He supposed he could get new glasses when he eventually reached Tucson. The fifty dollars was a small price to pay for his life. For a flash back there, he'd feared the bandit was going to shoot him.

The driver was shouting at them that Al Lane was shot and they were going back to Rosita. Benito Otero went forward then with the lieutenant and the drummer to help bring Lane down, feeling sorry for the wounded man. Going to California didn't seem very important now.

Chapter Twelve

Of late Evan Shelby had not tested his cough because he felt so well. However, with a twinge of overdue self-censure, he reminded himself that he must not neglect the practice. A year, Doc Renshaw had told him frankly, before he could be certain of his recovery. No matter how well he felt now, he must go the year.

Therefore, rising from his bed, he coughed into a blue bandanna, bringing up from deep in his lungs what little there was, and saw that he was still clear. Murmuring a fervent prayer of gratitude, he slid back the bar, opened the door, inhaled deeply, and gazed out on another day filled with limitless promise. Should he fall ill again, he had decided he would not undergo another long stretch of blasted hopes. The painful up-again, down-again struggle, the absolute draining of his spirit, and the grinding worry he caused his dear folks. Instead, he would end his life with the Colt .44. His will, provisions in detail, rested in William Keeley's safe at the store. If a lunger couldn't make it here, in this God-blessed valley, then it was not destined for him to make it elsewhere.

Sometime today he should keep his promise about the ride to Emory Pass and go into Rosita and ask Lucinda Holloway if tomorrow would be suitable for her. He had talked to Bear Webb and Silas Brown, who knew the region well, about reaching the pass.

He moved about his chores with relish, watering and feeding his horse, then sat down to another hearty breakfast. He made his bed and swept out the cabin and went out to the woodpile, splitting and sawing juniper and oak. Dark thoughts of self-destruction seldom came to him now. It was time to lift his sights. He'd never felt better. He was going to make it. It was something he sensed. An inner voice told him so. There was a life waiting for him. Lucinda Holloway had further kindled that hope, although he hardly dared think far into the future.

He was still at the woodpile, stacking lengths, when Dave Logan rode up.

"Step down," Evan said. "Come in. Good excuse for me to quit."

Logan tied up at the corral and walked slowly back. In his serious expression, Evan sensed more than a drop-by visit.

Then, with a break-through grin, the cowman said: "Hope you got some of that horse-soldier coffee left over from breakfast?"

"You bet. Come in."

Evan poured the coffee while Logan rolled a brown-paper cigarette and struck a match on a thumbnail. He took a deep drag, sipped, and said: "There's news in Rosita, but I'll start with what concerns me right now as a friend . . . what I've been hearin' in the Gem."

"What in the world?"

"It's Code Sloan. His tongue gets loose when he's drinkin', which is pretty often." He looked straight at Evan. "He's achin' to draw you into a gunfight."

"Any particular reason?"

"He's sayin' you're tellin' around town that you accused him of tryin' to steal your Spencer off the saddle."

"That's not true, though I would have felt within my rights to say so. Believe I'd told you that as I left the store, I saw him in the act of just about drawing the carbine. When I told him to hold on, he said he just wanted to look at it. I then said it was customary to ask permission to look at a man's carbine.

He challenged me, asked what I would do if he grabbed it. I told him I'd break his arm, and I meant it."

"What then?"

"We might have got into it right there, but Arch Kinder, who was with the rest of the crew in front of the store, called out to Sloan to ease off."

"Think Sloan would've taken the carbine if you hadn't happened to show up?"

"Positive. He'd've walked off with it. Later, remember, we had a few words in the saloon about what I'd said at the general meeting. Bear Webb saw what happened at the store. I haven't mentioned it to anyone else. In the first place, I don't see many people."

"And there ain't many to see."

"Now, what's the other news?"

"Well, day before yesterday, the westbound stage was robbed about five miles south of Rosita. Four masked riders. They killed Al Lane, the shotgun guard. Robbed the passengers. Lined 'em up. Pistol-whipped a miner for his bottle of whisky. Had to be damned good whisky for that."

Logan took another swallow of coffee and pinned a special look on Evan. "There's somethin' odd about the whole damn' robbery." He paused again, in a puzzled way."

"Odd?"

"Benito Otero was on the stage, bound for California. He said he had fifty dollars on him for expenses. They took that, then demanded the pay-off he got for the sale of his ranch. He was smart enough not to have it on him. Instead, he had a bank draft sewed inside his coat. Well, the bandit accused Benito of holdin' out on him. Made Benito empty all of his pockets. For a good while, Benito was afraid the bandit would shoot 'im. Finally, they rode off. Al Lane wounded one bandit."

Evan said: "That was close. Benito and I talked about the risk of carrying so much cash on his person. I went with him to see Mister Keeley about a bank draft. I left them with the understanding that's what Benito would do. Thank God, he did."

"That's not all about the hold-up. The main bandit's mask slipped, and Benito said he'd seen the man in town."

"Hope he's not telling that around?"

"Just Silas Brown and me. Silas warned him to keep his mouth shut. Benito is scared. He's stayin' with the Garzas. He'll leave on the next westbound."

"What about the wounded bandit? Did he show up at Doc Renshaw's?"

"Did yesterday morning. Doc patched him up. Told Silas he didn't know the man."

Both men held a contemplative silence, until Logan said: "Hell, it's about as plain as a mule's kick. Who else but Empire's riders did it? They all knew about Benito's money."

"I'd say most people in the valley know. Now, I wonder if Silas, as town marshal, will ride up to Empire's camp north of town to see if the wounded man is there?"

"He did yesterday afternoon. Only man there was the cook. He played dumb, as you'd expect."

"And the wounded man?"

"I'd say they hid 'im out somewhere. Or he vamoosed over the mountains, east to Hillsboro. Prob'ly not shot up too bad, from what Silas learned from Doc Renshaw."

"Which leaves Benito the only man on the stage who can identify the one bandit. We'd all better make sure he gets on that stage.'

"The Garzas will. I will, too. I'm closer than you are." Logan leaned back and fastened his attention on Evan. "Now, gettin' back to you and Code Sloan. Don't take him

144

lightly. He's a dangerous man."

"I won't."

"How fast are you with a gun?"

Evan raised a self-deprecating smile. "How fast is slow? I've never practiced. No need to."

"Strap on your gun belt and show me."

When Evan did so, Logan said: "Loosen your gun belt a notch or two. Let your gun hang a little lower, so it'll be closer to your hand. I've seen gunslicks hang their pistol around in front on their thigh in a cutaway holster where they could grab it faster. Not a bad idea, if a man's on the prod, advertisin' for a fight. . . . All right. Now draw your gun and cock it in the same motion."

Evan obeyed.

Logan frowned. "Reholster. Stand with your arms at your side. Now draw!"

Evan did, the Colt .44 feeling heavy. Suddenly he let out a disgusted laugh and casually stuck the revolver back in its holster.

Logan grinned. "You're not serious about this, Evan. Naturally, you're slow from lack of practice."

"It's no use. I'm no gunman."

"You're gonna have to learn. You have to protect yourself. I said Code Sloan is dangerous . . . he's also wild and unpredictable, which makes him more dangerous. He's killed men."

Evan was still skeptical. "You really think Sloan is out to get me, Dave? How ridiculous . . . over that carbine." He shook his head.

"I do. And as for you bein' slow on the draw, how do you think gunslicks get fast? Simple . . . they practice. They practice every day. *Every day,* pardner. How do I know? Why do you think I left Texas? I'm not wanted back there, no. But I killed two men in self-defense. Had enough of that. I left. There'd been more if I'd stayed . . . maybe Dave Logan next time. Too much pride involved . . . old feuds. Believe me, I know guns and I know about gunmen."

"I'm not doubting your word, Dave. I don't mean that."

Logan stood up. "Let's go outside and practice. Draw and shoot."

Evan followed him outside. Logan paced off a short distance to a juniper tree, came back, and said: "Now draw and fire at that tree."

Evan drew, fired, and the Colt leaped in his hand, the blast sounding unusually loud to him.

"You missed," Logan said, "but that's expected. Now start over. Practice till you empty your gun."

When Evan finished, Logan, nodding, went to the juniper and examined the bark. "One hit . . . that's not bad. Now, without loading, keep drawing and firing until I say halt."

Evan did as instructed, over and over. His hand was cramped when Logan finally called a halt.

"Now, do this every day, morning and afternoon, until you tire. You'll soon get faster, have a sure feel for your gun. Meanwhile, keep an eye out." Logan pushed a question at Evan with his eyes. "How often do you go into town?"

"Every Friday morning for my mail, maybe some groceries. Not that I get a letter every week. I also go just to see people. Visit a little."

"Might put that off for a while."

Evan held his gaze on Logan. "Dave, you went through a great deal in the war. You know what a letter means from folks back home, the simple enjoyment of seeing a loved one's handwriting. I'm not looking for trouble, but damned if I'll let Code Sloan prevent me from going into town when I please."

Logan grinned. "Aw, hell, I know how you feel. Just use judgment. Stay alert. Look around you. Watch your flanks, as they used to say. Remember this . . . if Sloan and the crew's loafin' out front on the boardwalk when you ride up, he might jump you." He glanced at the sun. "I'd better get along."

"I'm very much obliged to you, Dave, for warning me," Evan said, and held out his hand. "But wait. Want to show you something." He hastened to the cabin and returned with the Spencer carbine. Logan eyed him curiously.

"Watch," Evan said, facing the target juniper. He held the carbine down at his side. Then, with a flipping motion, he brought it up and eared back the hammer and fired. Juniper bark flew.

Logan's jaw dropped. "Hey! You did that one-handed. About as fast as your draw. Pretty good."

"Fact is," Evan explained, "I'm more used to the carbine than I am to the Colt. Handled it more."

Logan continued to regard him as if in a new light.

"But getting off only one shot in a face-to-face gunfight," Evan said, negatively shaking his head. "By the time I lowered the trigger guard to eject the empty case and bring up another shell from the magazine to the breech and eared back the hammer, I'd be a goner."

"Unless one shot was enough. I know the Spencer packs a wallop. What's the caliber?"

"Fifty-Two."

"That's a man-stopper."

"Or I could pack both the Colt and the carbine," Evan pondered.

"But which one would you go for? Wouldn't have much time. You couldn't stand there and scratch your head."

That broke Evan up, and Logan joined him in laughter.

"I believe an old saying applies here," Evan mused, "that, if a man goes where he's likely to run into trouble, chances are he will. Therefore, I'll stay clear of the Gem."

"Good idea. Unless I'm with you. Sloan will be there or out front."

"You make this sound inevitable, Dave."

"I'm just tryin' to warn you to be ready, if he comes at you. If whisky talk means anything." He turned to go. "Well. . . ."

Evan thanked him again and shook his hand.

Watching Logan ride off, he felt himself the fortunate recipient of an unusual endowment, of an ex-Confederate going out of his way to warn an ex-damnyankee. It made him feel warm all through and humbly grateful. A change, he thought, the valley had brought.

It was afternoon before he saddled and headed for Rosita. Now forewarned, he packed the Colt, but left the Spencer behind. He would include it next time he went for his mail. It followed that he would draw attention by taking it into the store, but he would not leave it on the saddle.

He admitted to himself that he felt some relief upon seeing the empty hitching racks at the store and the Gem when he rode into town. He particularly wanted no trouble today. He tied up at the hotel and entered, glad to see Hannah Young in her office.

After they exchanged greetings, he asked: "Miss Holloway in?"

"She is. Room Number One."

"Does she have company?"

"No. I'm sure she'll be glad to see you."

As he started to ascend the stairs, she said: "Heard the news about the stage hold-up?"

"Dave Logan told me this morning."

"Al Lane's funeral is pending."

"Too bad."

"I don't like the smell of all this, Captain."

"You mean . . . ?"

"I mean Empire's riders. I don't think Miss Holloway has linked it. And I'm sure not gonna tell her my suspicions, unless she asks me. She had nothing to do with hirin' that hardcase crew. Kinder brought 'em in."

"They should pull out when Miss Holloway has her ranch."

"She'll still need riders, though not as many, and Kinder will still be foreman." She motioned him in closer. "I'll tell you something, Evan. Over the years I've seen many men pass through this valley. Some good men wanted to stay, but couldn't . . . their past just a campfire behind them. They rode off, lookin' back. Some hardcases drifted in on the make. We gave them no welcome, so they rode on. But this cat-eyed Empire bunch will be here as long as Kinder is."

He listened with mounting interest.

"Things are comin' to a head," she said. "Miss Holloway let slip that she sent word back to Texas for an old friend named Hap McCoy to come out. Rode many years for her father."

"How do you see that?"

"She needs support and maybe trust." Shaking her head, Hannah said: "I don't mean she said that. She didn't. She's no leaner. She fights her own battles. Brought up that way. But sometimes everybody needs help."

Her voice cut off. Concern was suddenly evident in her face. He said—"Thanks for telling me, Hannah."—and left the room. Although the Code Sloan matter was his to work out, he sensed that it was also tied into the whole shebang.

He rapped lightly at the door designated Number One,

giving his name, and heard a surprised—"Oh!"—and then a warm—"Just a moment." In a short time, she unlocked and opened the door and said: "Please come in, Evan."

The locked door crossed his mind, but, after all, it was a hotel.

She held out her hand. Taking it, he felt the desire to embrace and kiss her, but held back. By then the moment was gone, and she was leading him to a chair. She looked mighty fetching in a neat print dress with a light blue-and-white pattern and a lace collar. Her hair, that she tied back when riding, fell in waves to her shoulders.

"Would you like to ride to Emory Pass tomorrow?" he asked.

"Still would."

"Fine. We should be back by late afternoon. Hope you can spare the time?"

"I have plenty of time on my hands now. Mister Conklin says it won't be long until we have enough range."

"And then," he said in a downcast voice, "you'll be leaving us."

"Don't make it sound so soon, Evan."

"Didn't mean to." In the ensuing gap of silence he felt that again he was venturing into uncharted waters, and he followed up cheerfully, insisting: "I could ask Hannah to fix us a lunch."

"Let me do that. Remember?"

"All right. And don't forget to bring your Henry, and I'll have my Spencer. And a canteen."

"The Henry goes whenever I ride. Same for a canteen. Beats cow tracks."

He smiled at that. "Good. I won't come for you at daybreak. I fear Missus Pettigrew would frown at that. Say, no later than eight. That all right?"

"You're talking to a ranch girl, Evan. My father used to say he had half his work done by that time."

Evan chuckled. "Then I'll make it a little earlier."

"Very good. I'll ask Bear Webb to have my horse saddled."

With a nod, he rose to go and said no more until he reached the door. "I'm, indeed, looking forward to our ride, Lucinda." Of a sudden he struck a formal pose. "How do you suppose Missus Pettigrew would phrase my calling on you in the morning?"

She picked it up at once, in a most proper voice. "Maybe like this. 'Never keep a lady waiting, sir. Always be prompt. *Always. Always, without fail.* If you cannot be prompt, sir, do not come at all.' "

He did a hunker in pretended fear and exited, laughing, while behind him he heard her pealing laughter as she locked the door.

He waved at Hannah on the way out. Mounting, he noticed two horses tied in front of the Gem.

Arch Kinder and Code Sloan came out of the saloon as Evan, thinking of the morrow, left town at a fast trot.

"There goes your man," Kinder reminded Sloan. "He's been in to see Miss Holloway."

"I can foller 'im right now and take 'im when he crosses the river," Sloan urged. "Easy. Like takin' candy from a baby."

"Won't do. Like I told you, you have to take him in front of others. You need witnesses, so it'll look like a fair fight. No other way will work . . . after you accuse him of callin' you a thief and spreadin' talk you tried to steal his saddle gun." *Sometimes,* Kinder thought, *you had to pound things into Code's whisky-soaked brain.*

Sloan looked greatly amused. "Reckon he'll deny it?"

"Shore he will."

"Then what?"

"You say he's callin' you a liar, and you open the ball. He'll have to draw, and you make an effort to defend himself."

"I'd rather take 'im right now. There's still time."

"Where's that old gravel in your gizzard?" Kinder knew how to swing Sloan his way: appeal to his vanity as a gunslinger. Sloan had killed an unknown number of men, but not as many as he bragged, which also went for the uncounted Indians and Mexicans. "Hell, Code, you're the fastest man I've ever seen with a gun, bar one. You have nothing to fear. Evan Shelby's a greenhorn with a gun."

"Easy to say, Arch, when you ain't doin' the fightin'."

"Well, Friday's the day. Get here early. You and some of the boys. That is, unless you aim to back out on your word." Kinder turned away as if to go to his horse.

"You know you can depend on me," Sloan hurriedly assured him.

Kinder went on a way before he looked around and said: "Shore, Code. Like old times. Let's have a drink, then I'll go courtin'."

Sloan soon left for camp, and Kinder, pleased with himself, quick-stepped in anticipation to the hotel. Always mindful of his manners before Mrs. Young, he doffed his hat to her, sitting in the office.

"Is Miss Holloway in, ma'am?"

"Believe she is, Mister Kinder."

Nodding his thanks, he took the stairs and, knocking politely at Number One, carefully pitched his voice to be courteous. "It's Arch, Lucinda. Need to talk to you about a downriver ranch."

There was no answer. He must have waited a full half minute, and still no answer. His mouth squeezing into a hard line, he knocked again and said: "Lucinda, it's Arch. Need to talk to you."

She did not answer. She wasn't going to answer. It stung his pride. His temper flared like a torch. He glared at the door, imagining her sitting calmly at the table, continuing to read a book, while she ignored him.

He had his feelings reined in enough when he passed the office to say to Mrs. Young—"Guess she's takin' a nap."—and left the hotel in a rage, his face set like granite.

Striding to his horse, he could feel his anger soaring ever higher. *A day is coming, Miss High and Mighty Lucinda, whether you like it or not. You can't do this to Arch Kinder. The ranch be damned . . . you're gonna know what a real man is like.*

Hannah Young remained motionless, still seeing the harsh cast of Kinder's face, thinking: *It's coming to a head, all right. It is. Faster than I thought.*

A looming fear for Lucinda took hold of her and kept rising. Well, as long as that sweet girl stayed in the Mimbres Hotel, Hannah Young would protect her as her very own. She kept an old six-shooter in a drawer, and she knew how to use it. Not long before Kinder showed up, Evan Shelby had gone to Lucinda's room, staying only a few minutes. Hannah could hear the pleasant tones of their voices, and their laughter when they parted. Shortly after that Lucinda had not responded to Kinder's repeated knock or voice, which told everything but why. It couldn't go on much longer. Kinder was Empire's foreman and not, Hannah sensed, the kind of man who would put up with that very long. Yet, Lucinda must have her reasons. It was troubling.

Lucinda watched from the window as Arch Kinder strode to his horse and mounted, jerking savagely on the reins, never mind a horse's tender mouth, and spurred into a hard run for camp.

She had seen him coming to the hotel, so had not been surprised. His new politeness hadn't fooled her. If she had let him in, she would have found herself warding him off. Next time she might not be able to. She just now remembered the Derringer, virtually useless in her handbag.

All at once a downdraft of feeling engulfed her. She fought back tears. *Hurry, Hap. Things are moving fast. We'll soon have the ranch. Then I'll need you by my side.*

She worried about him. What was delaying her old friend? Had something happened to him? Comanches? *Bandidos?*

She was thankful for tomorrow's ride to get her away from all this. At the cabin Evan had said he would come if she needed him, and he had come at a time that seemed almost uncanny, just when she had that need, not knowing what day he would say they might ride to Emory Pass. She had a quick stab of following guilt, fearing she might drag him into her troubles.

Her mind dwelled on him. For a held breath she had waited for him to hold her and kiss her on the lips, seeing the same desire in his face. Yet he had not, and she could only wonder why.

Chapter Thirteen

Up early next morning, Evan Shelby dutifully verified his good health, bent his head, and, speaking from his heart, thanked the Almighty, then watered and fed his horse.

After breakfast, he checked and loaded his weapons and saw to extra shells in the pockets of his jacket. Today the Spencer would also carry a load in the chamber, which made it an eight-shooter with seven in the magazine.

Next, heeding Dave Logan's warning, he practiced his draw. Was he any faster than when he first practiced? No, to be honest, he told himself. But he was getting a closer feel for the Colt revolver. He had handled and cared and fired the carbine so much over the years, it was almost an extension of himself as he flipped it up from his right side and eared back the hammer in that single motion.

When he trotted up to the Mimbres Hotel a little after seven, Lucinda's horse stood saddled at the hitching rail, the Henry rifle sheathed. Before he could step down, she came out and waved and mounted, Hannah Young behind her like a guardian mother hen. "Have a good time and be careful," she told them.

Evan nodded.

"Hannah's fixed us a big lunch," Lucinda said. "In my saddlebag."

He thanked Hannah, and then they were off, heading south down the river road, both horses moving into eager running walks.

Evan had not seen a more perfect New Mexico day. The

benevolent face of the sun in the perfect turquoise sky, the breeze curling along the valley, rustling in cadence the leaves of the lordly cottonwoods, the voice of the Mimbres, its sweet song never changing.

They rode in silence for a while, and, when they drew rein, she said: "I'm enjoying this so much, Evan. Everything. Plus, the feel of a good horse under you makes you feel good inside."

"I'm glad you're enjoying yourself. Maybe you needed an outing."

He thought she seemed about to say more before riding on.

Some two hours later they came to a trail that crossed the river and struck off into the mountains. They watered the horses, rested a while, saying little, and presently took the trail that was more like a narrow path for horses and pack mules than a way for wagons.

Climbing, they soon began to smell pines, and they halted and gave voice to further enjoyment, Lucinda speaking mostly in exclamations. Farther on, this far off the valley trail, deeper into the primitive wilderness of ponderosa pines and spruce and fir and stands of aspen, it was wise to ride more alertly. Evan did while she gazed about and indulged her pleasure. When they saw a lovely meadow not far off the trail, mantled with yellow and blue wildflowers, he saw her face glow almost child-like with the instant wish to go there, and he reined that way at once.

She could hardly wait to get down and start picking flowers. Upon grandly presenting one yellow and one blue to Evan, he bowed his head and stuck each in his hatband, then she swept off her hat and tucked a yellow one into her hair, posturing all the while.

"Gambol about," he said, "and you would pass for a nymph in the woods."

"Like this, maybe?" A flower in each hand, she skipped about while Evan laughed and applauded.

"Durn," he said, "if only I had a harp."

"We must not forget the horses," she said, and twined a flower in each mount's mane.

After that, they still lingered in the festooned meadow, hats off, soaking up the sun, watching the great sky and the pristine forest, while the horses lazily grazed, until, by unspoken assent, it was time to go.

"I know you must think I'm very silly sometimes," she remarked in a let-down way as they rode off.

"Not a bit," he countered, "after all, you danced divinely."

That broke her momentary mood. Laughing, she said: "You can always make me see the light side, Evan."

"Furthermore," he insisted, shaking an instructive forefinger, "harp music went with your dance. I want you to know, Miss Holloway, that your intrepid guide once played the violin. Well, briefly, until my suffering and honest teacher sent a note home to my mother, saying it was a waste of money, which could be better spent on the poor."

"But why?" she asked, looking concerned.

"Well, I would be there sawing away, while all the time, through the open window, I'd hear my friends playing baseball. I couldn't concentrate. On top of that, later, I never made the team, either."

"Oh," she said, pouting her lips with pretended sympathy, "it's such a sad story of wasted talent."

Chuckling outright at her performance, he gave her a playful poke on the shoulder. "You got me," he said. "Now we're even."

The sun was straight overhead when they arrived at Emory Pass, before them an unlimited view of mountains, and more mountains far beyond, leaving them spellbound in silence.

"Oh, my," she marveled. "It's so beautiful and vast, stretching on and on."

"After the Mexican War," he said, "the people in Washington wondered what the nation's newly acquired land was like from the Río Grande to the Pacific. So the Army sent a Lieutenant William Emory out here with a party. Being a topographical engineer, he made maps, studied the land and the rivers, took readings of the stars. Thanks to him, Miss Lucinda Holloway of Southwest Texas knows exactly where she is at this moment."

She turned to look at him, pleased with what he had just said, making a picture framed before him with her hat off, light-brown hair windblown across her forehead, and the sun like balm on her face. Now and then, near her, he caught the delightful scent of violets.

"It's so beautiful from up here," she said reverently. "A sight to remember. How high do you suppose we are?"

"Above eight thousand. I read the lieutenant's report in an engineering class before I was posted at Fort Craig before the war."

Hunger took over, and during lunch, with the Henry and the Spencer at hand, they continued to enjoy the endless distance. Afterward, as if this was a particular day they wanted to prolong, they moved to a great flat rock that provided a vista and sat and chatted and delayed leaving. Time fled. Their talk gradually lapsed into thoughtfulness.

Evan, keeping an eye on the head of the trail, knew they had to leave before long. He caught her elusive pensiveness again. She was still hurting over her father, but, being a Holloway, she'd say nothing. Sensing that, he longed to ease her young sorrow, but felt at loss as to how. As a senior officer in the war, he often had tried to comfort young boys in his command who had lost a close friend in battle or had just suffered the wrenching loss of a family member back home. Sometimes a warm hand on a slumped shoulder was all that could be done; yet, it was one man reaching out to another.

"Growing up," he began, "I used to hear it said . . . mostly by old women, I think now . . . that time heals all wounds and troubles. Ever hear that, Lucinda?"

"I suppose so," she said, a little surprised at the question.

"Well, I don't agree with that."

Which stirred her to rest her attention full on him.

"What time does," he said, "is it allows us to accept our loss, which we sorely need. It allows us to face it. But it also gives us faith and hope, which we sorely need. It also leaves us strength through good memories. That's the way it is to me, and we have to go on . . . and you are doing that, I know." Then, suddenly, he added: "But if you need someone to talk to, Lucinda . . . as we all do sometimes . . . I'm a good listener." He paused. "And I do feel for you."

Her eyes closed in such a certain way that absolutely sent his senses reeling. She said—"Oh, Evan."—and came to him with open arms, and he saw she was waiting for him to kiss her. Instead, he held her close and kissed her face again and again as he took in the sweet scent of her, then pulled away. He said: "There's something I have to tell you, Lucinda."

She drew back, fear leaping into her eyes. "What is it?"

"I'm a lunger," he said flatly, and looked down. "I know you've wondered why I'm way out here. I came out for my health, to live or die. But I haven't coughed blood for seven months."

"That's wonderful!"

"Yes. I feel wonderful. But Doc Renshaw, himself once a lunger, says I have to wait a year to be sure. That's why I didn't kiss you on the lips. My God, I want to! I can't till then.

I have to be sure. You see, Lucinda, I love you very much."

"And I love you, Evan. Very much. I've known for some time."

She kissed him on both bearded cheeks and pushed back a lock of hair from his forehead and stroked his face and looked into his eyes. He hadn't remembered taking off his hat, but he had.

Still looking into his eyes, she said: "You are always very sweet to me, Evan. Always smiling. You always make me feel free and happy just being around you. You make me feel like a woman, too," she added, coloring a little, and then added in a somber vein: "Yes, I've felt lonely. I hope you haven't lost any loved ones."

"My only brother, who was younger . . . died at Atlanta. It almost killed my mother. In the Army I lost close friends . . . that was the terrible damned war. Both sides lost so much. Many of them mere boys. We must never let our country fight divided again." He kept holding her as he talked, while she looked at the pain in his face with understanding. "War changes a man forever. I saw its havoc repeated over and over. Sometimes such scenes sweep across my mind, still as vivid as when they occurred. Sometimes they disturb my sleep. But most times I keep them at a distance. A solitary man must stay busy. So, as you know, I read or walk or clear out the trail, and there's always my woodpile. It all helps me sleep at night." He looked off and back, his eyes trailing over her face. "I didn't want to stray so far," he said, and smiled.

And then, he found her face against his, and she was saying: "Do you know when I first began to love you?"

"You mean, when was the most fortunate day of my life?"

"That day at the votive spring. When you gave me the blue turquoise. I knew then."

"I sensed myself something happening that day . . . a sort

of wonder . . . but was afraid to admit it, knowing I shouldn't."

She looked at him. "Mexican women who raised me taught me reverence for God. I felt it that day where the Forgotten Ones had lived so long ago and made their simple but beautiful offerings. Everything seemed so clear and true to me that day. I felt so thankful for all things, and for another reason," she concluded, looking at him.

"A man could be so fortunate," he said, and kissed her tenderly.

They held each other for a long, long time, seldom speaking, locked in their special silence, gazing off, held by the vista, until at last he roused himself and judged the sun, saying: "We must go, Lucinda. Ride when we can see. Get out of the woods before dark."

Rising, they embraced and held long cheek kisses, went to the horses, sheathed their weapons, and mounted.

They turned down the rough trail at a slow trot into the forest and its cathedral coolness. Evan did not ride hurriedly. In country this vast a principal trail, although seldom traveled, was where one would most likely run into trouble, but then most likely not at all. Some distance from the pass, scanning the trail, he pointed downward. "Unshod tracks came in from the west after we passed and turned down the trail. Look sharp."

She nodded.

"We're all right," he assured her.

Now they proceeded at a reconnoitering walk, side by side. Once he halted and canted his head, listening intently— just bird song and the purring wind. They rode on. With the lowering sun, long shadows were stealing into the lofty timber.

When an owl hooted beyond them down the trail, Evan

halted immediately and looked at her. "Owls hoot at night," he said. "Not daytime."

"What does it mean?"

"It's a signal. Apaches used it on us more than once out of Fort Craig. See down the trail here where it makes a sharp bend?"

"Oh, yes."

"They've very likely set up an ambush there. So we're going to take a flanking movement off to our right, slip around 'em, and circle in on the trail well below the bend. Now, you pull over and ride on my right. Stick close. Rifle ready." So saying, he drew the Spencer.

She did as he said, and, at a walk, they quit the trail and angled off quietly into the forest. It seemed very hushed and waiting all around them now, save for the muted cadence of hoofs on carpeted pine needles. Lucinda seemed a mite pale, but alert as she trailed her eyes back and forth, while holding the Henry across her arms. He pressed her shoulder for reassurance.

Evan focused his attention on the vicinity of the bend to his left. He caught indistinct movement there among the trees and brush, which told him enough, and which he hoped remained there, undisturbed by their quiet passage. Thus, his interpretation of the incoming horse tracks, based on the past, still held true. Otherwise, they would have ridden right into it.

Going on, holding to a walk, swiveling his gaze from the bend to their front, he was beginning to think they were in the clear, when it happened without warning, with a startling suddenness, with Lucinda gasping: "Evan, look!" And before them on another narrow path that fed into the main trail from the west loomed an Apache, traveling at a swinging dog-trot. For an instant he was as astonished as they.

Evan shot him just as the warrior was jerking his rifle upward, getting off a wild shot. The Apache broke down as if kicked, black eyes wide with amazement, clutched his chest, and did not get up.

"Come on! Stick close!"

Evan led them on at a fast trot, weaving through the crowded trees. On the trail back at the bend a commotion was taking place—much shouting and the trampling of horses. If a white man could ever figure out what Apaches would do, he thought they would rush to where they'd heard the shots. A brief distraction, but enough time to reach the trail going on south to the river.

In what seemed like a long time, although Evan knew it was only minutes, they came to the trail. Looking back, he saw the way was still clear. Turning, he caught Lucinda's look of relief, and he nodded again and again. From there he took them on at a gallop, while constantly checking their back trail.

To his dread, he sighted them much sooner than expected. A knot of riders coming like fury itself, screeching and flailing their fleet mounts. Some ten or more. He knew the two of them couldn't go on this way. Couldn't outrun them.

Seeing his sudden concern and the reason why, she flinched and looked at him with questioning eyes.

"Hold up," he said. "We have to stop 'em."

By the time they had used precious moments pulling up and reining around, their pursuers appeared no less than some three hundred yards away, still coming at a dead run.

"You take the lead rider on your side," he instructed her. "I'll take the left side. Take aim! Ready! Fire!"

Their mounts jerked at the crashing sounds, but held steady. Powder smoke bloomed, acrid to the nose.

He glimpsed a rider jerking sideways off his horse, and another horse crippling away with its rider.

But instead of slowing, the other Apaches charged as before, a howling mass.

"Evan," she said, uncertain.

"We're all right! They're coming on because they're used to facing single-shot muzzleloaders!" He was barking at her, fearing for her. "Pick a target now! Ready! Aim! Fire! Keep firing!"

He was counting his shots as he sighted and blasted away, jaws clenched. She was firing steadily, not wildly. He heard the whine of ricocheting bullets. Once he thought he heard a nearby snipping sound. When he ceased firing with two rounds left, she also quit, and through the lifting fog of powder smoke he saw that they had, indeed, halted the charge. Three riders were out of it completely, strung along the trail. One sitting up, head down. Another sprawled. Another crawling. Two horses were down. The other Apaches milled about.

"Come on! Let's go!" he yelled at her, and they took off together.

Again, the hard galloping and looking back. Not yet running the horses all out, Evan believed they had to save something back if it got tighter. When he checked up again after a while and looked back, the trail was clear, and he heaved a great sigh of relief.

"Let's reload."

They pulled up. He drew the Spencer's magazine from the butt stock, fed in five shells, reinserted the magazine, and locked it, then added another shell in the chamber.

As she finished reloading the Henry magazine under the barrel and turned, he saw a small ragged tear in the side of her hat.

"My God!" he said, aghast. "Are you hurt?"

"No, I'm all right."

"You sure? A bullet's ripped your hat! Let me see. Take off your hat."

Still shaken, he brushed at her hair with fumbling fingers, afraid he'd find blood, afraid she was in a daze. To his immense relief, there was no blood. He kissed her hair tenderly. Still, he bent her a sharp look of concern.

"I did feel a little tug," she said.

Self-blame smote him, sick at heart how close she had come to injury, possibly death, yet so utterly thankful she had escaped. He was treating her as a comrade today. How else could he? She had not faltered once, brave as could be. Together they had stopped the charge. Could he have done it alone? He wasn't sure. Her Henry out-ranged his short-barreled Spencer considerably, which had made a telling difference. He thought: *Rip Holloway's daughter.*

"Let's go," he said. "This time you ride ahead of me."

"But I want to ride beside you, Evan."

"Lucinda, please do as I say. I can't have you hurt. I couldn't stand it. Ride ahead. Stay low in the saddle. We're all right."

Without another word, she rode ahead.

Grimly determined to protect her, he fell in directly behind her, shielding her, the horses traveling at a gallop. Mindful of the one Apache that had surprised them trotting into their trail, he kept up a constant vigilance all around.

For an interval they seemed to ride through a lull. An uneasy lull. From the past, he knew Apaches did not give up easily. Here, they knew the forest. Scouting out of Fort Craig, he had learned to expect the unexpected just when a detachment assumed there was no threat.

He jerked at the blur of horse movement across the meadow to his left at the edge of the timber He halted, searching, waiting.

Suddenly he found Lucinda at his side, rifle ready.

"I saw horses move in the timber on the far side of that meadow," he said, pointing.

Nothing changed while he spoke. And then he could see horses taking bold shape in the timber. In moments riders burst into view, bent low.

"They're at about eight hundred yards," he said crisply. "Beyond carbine range. Adjust your sights. Pick the lead riders."

She fired two quick rounds without visible effect.

"Take your time," he said. "They're ridin' low. So shoot the horses. If they get much closer, I'll start firing. We're all right."

As he spoke, a horse broke down, dumping its rider. Then another horse stumbled, losing its rider. One unhorsed Apache got up, then fell. A horse buck-jumped, dragging a leg. She shot the rider off. A wounded horse bolted, smashing into two charging horses, knocking one rider off his mount.

That scattered the lead riders and broke the momentum of the charge.

Now Evan started firing, just barely within carbine range. Lucinda did not let up. Together they maintained a steady rate of fire.

It was soon over, the riders drawing away, broken. More unhorsed. Several lay scattered.

"I don't think we'll see this war party again," he said, and threw an arm around her. "You did mighty well. Now, let's get the hell out of here!"

"May I accompany you side by side, Captain Shelby, formerly brevet Major Shelby?"

He had hurt her feelings back there, although he knew he had taken the right precautions. Only by the grace of God had she been spared. A few more inches. . . . He grinned at her.

"My pleasure, Miss Holloway. Captain Shelby, formerly brevet Major Shelby, is humbly at your service, believe me."

It was dusk when they reached the singing river and watered the tired horses and without delay crossed to the winding river road. Side by side, saying little, because little needed to be said, often touching each other, a brushing kiss now and then, the horses perking up because feed always awaited them after a day's long ride.

When Rosita's few pallid lights broke the early evening ahead of them, Evan said: "I am going to take you right to Hannah's doorstep. I know she'll be anxious and waiting."

Hannah had hung a lantern on the verandah. At the sound of horses she rushed out of the hotel, her voice carrying: "Are you all right?"

"We're fine," Evan said. "Lucinda's fine. Trouble on the trail coming back . . . Apaches. Tell you about it later."

They tied up, and, when Lucinda stepped up on the verandah, Hannah hugged her again and again. "Everybody's been worried. Bear and Silas just left. They were gonna form a posse, if you hadn't come in by morning."

She gave Evan an enveloping hug. "I'll tell you this, Hannah," he said. "Miss Lucinda Holloway is a girl to ride the mountains with."

Hannah became very busy. "Come in here! The supper I'd planned is still warm. Coffee first. Sit down. And, Lucinda, don't you try to help as usual. You stay right there, young lady."

Laughing, Lucinda said: "It just occurs to me that I haven't been able to get in a word. You and Evan are doing all the talking."

"That's all right," Hannah said. "Now's the time to eat and rest. You can talk later."

"I'd better take care of the horses first," Evan said, and left.

Bear Webb met him at the livery entrance. "Heard y'all ride up and was just comin' over. Miss Holloway all right?"

"She's fine," Evan said, and briefly told him what had happened.

"That bend in the trail has caught many an unlucky traveler. You two were plumb lucky."

"I realize that. It scares me to think about it now. She was cool with that long-range Henry. No man could have done better."

"That don't surprise me none. As Silas says, she was brought up right."

After Hannah's usual generous supper and much coffee, they sat in the office and talked.

"I must tell you," Evan said in a confessional tone, "that a bullet nipped Lucinda's hat. Rather, a fragment from a ricochet. It almost took my mind away when I saw the rip. So we were lucky. Thank God many times over."

"Oh, my," said Hannah.

When Lucinda began to nod, Evan got up, saying: "I'd better go. It's not far to the cabin."

Hannah glared at him. "You'll do no such thing, Evan Shelby! Number Three is available. Clean sheets. A pitcher of water, towels, and soap. You have to stay here tonight."

"Yes, Evan," Lucinda pleaded, fatigue showing in her eyes. "You must. No more riding tonight."

He smiled at them both. "Gladly overruled, ladies. Thank you, Hannah. You don't have to remind me about clean sheets."

He was about to leave something unfinished, but he looked at Lucinda and their eyes met. He went to her, and she stood up, and he put his arms around her.

"Hannah," he said, "it's important we tell you the rest of today's story. Lucinda and I love each other . . . we said so today. First, I told her I'm a lunger . . . but cough-free for seven months. Never felt better. Doc Renshaw says a person should go a year to make certain. I believe I'll make it."

Hannah's eyes were glistening. "I've seen this coming. I'm so happy for you. You're both like family. Lucinda is like a daughter."

She hugged them both amid tears.

Chapter Fourteen

After a late breakfast, Evan Shelby went to the livery and led his horse back to the hotel. Lucinda was waiting on the verandah.

"Evan," she said, looking up at him, "I am so happy. I feel so blessed."

"It would take a poet to express how I feel, and, since I'm not a poet," he said, smiling, "all I can say is I'm as happy as any man could possibly be, and so thankful I brought you back unhurt. It still scares me. Things can happen so fast in an open fight like that. A person can be bleeding a little at first and not realize it. Then it gets very bad, and they pass out." He shook off the thought. "Well. . . ." He kissed her on the forehead as tenderly as one might a small child, then on the cheek, and embraced her.

"When will I see you again?" she asked, looking somber.

"Soon. Let's see. What day is this?"

"Wednesday."

"Wasn't quite sure. Days hardly register on me sometimes."

"It is Wednesday."

He chuckled. "Thanks. I have some chores to do around the cabin. Split and stock wood. Work on the corral. And I just ordered some horse feed from Silas. He can't bring it out till either late tomorrow morning or afternoon. But I promise I'll come in Friday morning to see you. It's also my mail day."

"That's better than Saturday."

"Tomorrow would be better, but there's the horse feed."

"And you must not forget your horse."

He held up his right hand. "I, Evan Shelby," he said with mock solemnity, "swear that I will not forget my horse. Neither will I forget to feed my horse."

"That's much better. I can't have my favorite cavalryman forgetting his faithful horse" She kissed him then on the cheek.

"What about you, here? I mean the ranch."

"I'll go to the land office today and find out what's going on. I do all my business there now." He held back the impulse to ask her why. However, she saw it in his eyes and said: "It's more business-like."

He agreed with a nod. "Look," he said, "I'll be in and out from now on. But if you need me and I'm not around, tell Silas or Bear. I want to help you, Lucinda."

"You've already helped me, Evan. I see things now that I didn't see before. Maybe I've grown up."

She was so serious he took her hand. "You proved yesterday you had already grown up, believe me. You're a mighty brave girl and very dear."

"To be honest, I confess I was very frightened. All the hideous yelling and horses charging. The gunfire."

"But you didn't panic. In battle, all men feel fright at times. If they didn't, they wouldn't be human. But the brave ones stay and fight. You did that. Now, I'll let you in on a little secret . . . I felt fear, too." Giving her a big smile, he added: "I'm mighty proud to ride with you, Miss Holloway." He kissed her, then whispered in her ear: "You are my sweetheart, you know."

Rather quickly, he mounted and reined away, calling: "See you Friday morning."

Until Friday, she thought. *It will seem like a very long time.*

She watched his cavalryman's figure, tall and straight in the saddle, until he faded from view on the river road, and continued to watch for long moments before turning to go inside. She missed him already.

"Miss Holloway."

She looked around. It was William Keeley. She hadn't noticed him hurrying across the street. He held a letter.

He was most cordial. "I want to say how glad I am to hear that you and Captain Shelby are safe. With so many peaceful days here along the Mimbres, we in Rosita forget that Apaches can still be a threat. I say again . . . I am most thankful you are both safe."

"Thank you, sir. You are very kind. It was quite an experience for me. Captain Shelby knew what to do and protected me in every way. Fortunately we were well armed. His Spencer carbine and my Henry rifle."

"The Henry. Now there is a real Western rifle. Sixteen shots. After what happened, I may order a few more. But I'm straying from my other reason for seeing you." He raised his hands in apology, his round, genial face ringed with the white beard, beseeching and compelling. "This letter came for you last week," he confessed. "Somehow it got put back with some business letters, and I just found it this morning. Here it is, delivered late with my many apologies. The first letter I've misplaced in years. I'm very sorry, Miss Holloway. I hope you'll forgive me."

Returning him a forgiving smile, she took it, saying: "I'm sure a few days won't matter, Mister Keeley. Thank you very much for bringing it over."

One look at the postmark told her enough. She opened it anxiously, fearing bad news. Written in Hap McCoy's cowpuncher's scrawl, it read succinctly:

Dear Miss Lucinda,
    Shorty fell with me. Left me stove up. That horse

stepped in a gopher hole. Feeling better. Both of us.
I will be there with my guns, as you asked.

Your old friend,
Hap McCoy

She felt like celebrating and gave a genuine cowboy whoop
and stamped her booted feet. Shorty was a mouse-colored
dun, a grulla, Hap's favorite cow horse. Dear, lovable old
Hap. So dependable. He was family. About the same age as
her father. From the same school of tough times—true
Texans fighting Comanches, rustlers and outlaws, and the al-
ways-threatening *bandidos* slipping across the border on fast
horses. Once, when she asked Hap to tell her about some of
the experiences he and her father had gone through in the
early days, he had summed up simply: "We rode together,
fought together, got drunk together, and went hungry together. If one got in a little personal trouble, the other one
was always there. *Compadres.*" Hap had been terribly shaken
at her father's death, had kept to himself, locked in his grief,
except to comfort her. An old bachelor, he had no family
now, but her. Meanwhile, Arch Kinder had pushed in with a
shoulder to cry on.

Why hadn't her father made Hap the *segundo* instead of
Arch Kinder? It was not the first time she had asked herself.
Hap knew cattle, horses, grass, and water. Everything. Then
why? Had he been so used to having Hap around that he saw
his easy-going old friend as less a man to take that responsi-
bility? Hap was a peacemaker first, gun play his last resort,
because he was a gentle man at heart. In addition, he got
along with Mexican *vaqueros* and their families, treated them
with respect and understanding, which they returned. An impatient man, Arch forced issues with scant delay. He looked
down on Mexicans, treated them as inferiors. But he was

showy and strong and looked impressive. Perhaps her father, thinking ahead, had decided that Arch, younger than Hap, was the wisest choice for his daughter's future benefit. Knowing her father, she sensed that had been his thought.

Hap was coming. That was what mattered now. She felt a fresh surge of confidence about handling ranch matters and firing Arch Kinder as *segundo* when all hell would break loose, which it surely would. She had no other choice. She was going on trusted instinct. Further, she knew now that Arch Kinder was the rider she had caught watching her after she left Evan's cabin. Had to be.

It was Thursday afternoon in the Gem.

Arch Kinder arrived after the crew and, nodding at Code Sloan, took a table away from the others. He signaled Cap Shaw for drinks as Sloan joined him. When Sloan downed his whisky without pause, Kinder scowled and cautioned him: "Don't forget you've got a job to do tomorrow. Go easy on the hard stuff."

"I can handle it. I know my limit. Until then, I drink."

Kinder let a politic smile edge into the corners of his mouth. "Just what is your limit, Code?" He didn't want to rile the gunman, just keep him fit.

"What I say it is."

"Granted, you handle your whisky better than most. An average cowboy would fall flat on his face tryin' to keep up with you."

Code Sloan grinned at the observation, proud of his capacity.

Enough said on the matter, Kinder decided. In a casual way, he remarked: "Reckon you heard about Apaches jumpin' Miss Holloway and the Yankee captain up in the mountains yesterday?"

"Just heard Cap Shaw mention it. What all happened?"

"They got back all right. Thanks to her long-range Henry rifle and his Spencer carbine."

"That god-damned carbine. It's still in my craw . . . that day."

"Shelby's the big hero around town, you know," Kinder said, his voice dripping sarcasm.

Sloan had to laugh at him. "Gripes your gut, don't it? Him savin' Empire's purty owner from Apaches. Him, the big hero."

Kinder took affront. "Expect me to like it?"

"If he hadn't saved her, you'd be outta work with the rest of us."

"Damned right I'm glad she's safe. God, yes!"

Sloan threw him a strange look, as if seeing Kinder in a much different light than usual. Their talk fell away; the silence grew. After Kinder signaled for more drinks, Sloan said: "I keep wonderin' why the stage hold-up went wrong. Why the old man didn't have the ranch pay-off on 'im."

"I'll tell you why," Kinder replied at once. "It was Shelby's fault. He advised the old man to get a bank draft. Not carry all the cash on his person."

"How do you know that?"

"Keeley told me. Was sayin' what a smart idea it was. But he said who would think the stage would be robbed? That was the first stage hold-up ever on the Mimbres River road."

Sloan threw down his whisky with a jerk of his arm so abruptly that Kinder stared at him.

"I been thinkin' how us boys took chances. Jess gittin' shot. Me, foremost, as I shook down the passengers. Any one of 'em coulda plugged me with a hide-out gun."

"The chances a man takes in that game," Kinder reminded him, his tone skirting indifference, now sounding like the old Arch Kinder to Sloan. Not the one concerned for Miss Holloway.

"Chances!" Sloan repeated. "Chances I'll be takin' tomorrow when I challenge the Yank." He got into Kinder's face. "Five hundred won't do it, Arch. You have to pile the stack higher . . . another five hundred or ol' Code Sloan don't play the game this time around!"

"What?" Kinder's voice was so loud other riders glanced his way, and he lowered it. "You're tryin' to hold me up, go back on your word. You can't do that to me, Code."

"Like hell, I can't! Just gittin' a little smarter is all, Arch. I take the chances as always. Now, for a change, you pay what's fair or it's off."

"You can't back out on me now!"

Sloan lurched to his feet and would have gone, but Kinder said: "Hold on, god dammit! Let's powwow a little. I'll make it six."

Sloan sat down, but looked away. "You heard me. Another five."

"I positively won't do that. I'll make it eight hundred with a hundred of that on the barrelhead right now. That's all I've got on me. I've already paid you a hundred."

"Yeah. Chicken feed."

Under the table, Kinder took greenbacks from a wallet.

"Well, all right," Sloan said, taking the money.

"All the rest of it tomorrow night. Meanwhile, stay sober."

That settled, Kinder left and stood on the boardwalk in front of the saloon, reviewing what had just taken place. Sloan had got to him for that extra money, but it would be worth it. If by some quirk, Sloan lost the gunfight, Kinder knew of a killer for hire in Tucson he could contact by the next weekly stage west, assuming the man was not on a mission. A sure operator, this *hombre*—mysterious Henry Hewitt

176

Birdwell, widely known as a quick-draw artist, without a doubt the fastest gun in the Southwest. A few kill-crazy gunslicks had challenged him just to find out; none had survived. His services were expensive, as expected. But he never failed, so the legend ran. Lived quietly. Yet available, if you knew how to contact him, which Kinder did, knowing certain people along the border who had used his services. He killed quickly and left quietly, cash in hand.

Gazing across at the Mimbres Hotel, he thought of Lucinda Holloway. No use going over there; she wouldn't see him. Only at the office. That burned his innards, the worst insult to his vast pride. Yet it amused him that he was using unlimited Empire acreage money to pay Sloan to kill Evan Shelby. If Sloan failed, he would use more of her money to bring in Birdwell, who had never failed. With Shelby out of the way, Miss Lucinda might very well find herself looking more favorably on Arch Kinder, needing him and his experience to run her ranching operations here and in Texas. That would help make up for the times he had lurked like a stalker in the river timber, jealousy and hate for Shelby consuming him, while he had watched for her to return from Shelby's place.

Well, Friday, Kinder reflected, he would be here watching. This time for another and final purpose.

Chapter Fifteen

Anticipation of the day ahead aroused Evan Shelby earlier than usual. He checked his cough, said his fervent prayer of gratitude, ending with a loud "Amen." Next he started a juniper fire in the little stove, cared for Dan, his horse, ate a hearty breakfast, brought in stove wood, and, because he was going to see Lucinda today, poured hot water into a wash pan, took a cavalryman's bath from head to toe, and trimmed his beard. He needed a wooden washtub, but had held off, since Josefa Garza did his laundry.

It was remarkable, he thought, what a man could do with so little water while out on scout and stay passably clean;, otherwise, he'd smell like a Bulgarian bandit, which he likely would anyway. He had an entire creek at hand, and he used it liberally, but old and frugal bachelor habits still largely governed his attention to himself. The secret was plenty of scrubbing and good soap. He'd better get that washtub.

His last duty was to check the Colt Army .44 revolver and the Spencer, seeing to a cartridge in the carbine's chamber, ready to fire. Although he had faith in the Colt, he realized that he lacked the hand speed required against a quick-draw gunman like Code Sloan. However, he thought, a man could make up for part of that by making certain his first shot hit home. For practice and feel, he drew the revolver until he tired of it, then the same for the Spencer, flipping it up. Indeed, it felt easy in his hand; as for speed, he couldn't say.

Now it was time to go.

It was about ten o'clock when he saddled into Rosita. As he tied up at the hotel, he spied Lucinda at her window, evidently waiting for him. He waved and pointed to the store where he would pick up his mail, and she waved and threw him a kiss.

But all at once he caught the change in her face when he unsheathed the Spencer and started across the street. Before him everything began to register fast. The Gem's hitching rack was full. Empire's riders, he'd bet. At the same time a man suddenly left the bench on the boardwalk in front of the saloon and stepped inside. A look-out? Setting the stage? Only a few horses tied at the store.

The Gem was noisy and profane as usual. Common sense told him he wasn't going in there and place himself at a disadvantage.

The instant he entered the store, Dave Logan came up to him so fast Evan knew that his friend had been watching and waiting for him.

"What are you doing in town this time of week?" Evan teased him.

"Had to check my mail. Thought maybe some of my old broken-hearted sweethearts I left back in Texas would be writin' me again, beggin' me to come back."

"Well, did you hear anything?"

"No, dang it."

"Maybe next week."

Suddenly the banter left the cowman's leathery face. "Listen, Evan, I'm afraid this is gonna be the day. I drop by the Gem enough to catch the drift o' things, an' what Cap Shaw lets drop. Want you to know that I aim to back you up if you get jumped."

"Aw, thanks, Dave. But I don't want you to get involved.

It's my fight. I'll have to handle it."

"That's the rub. I'm afraid you can't." He looked right at Evan, his mouth grim. "You don't realize what you're up against."

"I'm not damn' fool enough to go into the Gem looking for it."

"On the other hand, it may come lookin' for you."

"You mean Code Sloan, of course?"

"Who else?"

"What could get into a man to kill another over a little wrangle about a carbine? Pride, maybe?"

"You'd be surprised how little it takes. Mix that with too much whisky and there's a gunfight. Whisky led to many a killin' back in Texas where I came from. Why they call it brave-maker. Sloan an' all the Empire riders are tankin' up right now . . . started early." As Evan shook his head in disbelief, Logan added ominously: "Another whisky whisper says money."

"Money? Just how?"

"There may be money behind this to get you killed."

"Now, that is hard to believe. Whose money?"

"The whisper faded out right there, like the *hombre* spillin' the beans, an Empire hand, who had already said too much. But it's obvious Sloan is throwin' money around, more'n usual."

Evan shook his head. "This amazes me more and more. I thank you for warning me, Dave." He slapped Logan on the back. "I'll get my mail and drop by the hotel."

William Keeley stood close by. "I couldn't help overhearing, Captain. Dave is right. You've got to be on guard today."

"I intend to. Thank you. Do I have any mail?"

"No letters, I recall. Let me make sure." Keeley hurried

behind the post office counter and, shortly, handed Evan a rolled-up newspaper. "That's all." He kept his eyes on the front doorway as he said: "I don't like the atmosphere around here this morning. It's heavy, like something's about to drop. I told Cap Shaw to slow down the drinks, if possible. Empire is a hard-drinking, quarrelsome lot." Then he looked at Logan and back to Evan. "There's a saddled horse out back, Captain. You take it and ride away from this and not a word will be said from here. I'll have your mount taken to the livery. Why don't you do that, Captain?" He was more than suggesting.

"Yes," Logan said, "get outta here, Evan."

"If I run now, I'll have to run again, say next time in town. And keep on running whenever Empire's in."

"At least ride out today," Keeley urged. "Let this simmer down."

Evan played it all through his mind, back and forth, seeing how the threat would still persist if he ran. No end to it as long as Empire was in the valley. He couldn't go on that way. He had come out here to live or die, and, having made his way this far on the road to regaining his health, he was not going to compromise, to cheapen himself. And there was Lucinda. He thought she would understand why he had run, but wouldn't he be less a man in her eyes as well as his own?

"I thank you men," he said, "but I can't do it. I would just be putting off what has to be faced eventually."

There came the rising hum of voices from outside and the clump of boots on the boardwalk. Logan stepped to a front window and looked toward the Gem. "They're comin' outside," he said, turning to Evan. "Waitin' for you to come out." He looked again and said: "The whole damned outfit. Includin' Arch Kinder and that flap-mouthed salesman, Conklin. Like a stage play, Evan, waitin' for the main character to come out." He wheeled around. "Go grab that horse, Evan. Get the hell outta here this one time!"

Quite deliberately Evan laid the rolled newspaper on a stack of boxes, shook his head, took a deep breath, and started for the doorway, the Spencer hanging low in his right hand.

Logan, fast on his feet, beat Evan to the door. "Don't be a damn' fool, Evan. You don't have to go out there to prove anything today. There's always tomorrow, and a fairer fight. Code Sloan may not be the only one gunnin' for you."

"It has to be this way," Evan said. "A man runs once, he'll have to run again or fight. I'd rather fight now."

Logan stared hard at him. Gradually a reluctant admission rose to his eyes. "I guess so" he said, and moved aside. "Only I'm goin' out that door with you."

"Remember, it's my fight," Evan said, and cocked the Spencer's hammer.

"Good," said Logan, seeing that.

The instant Evan came out on the boardwalk, Logan a step behind him, the voices ceased and every eye seemed to focus on him.

"There he is," a voice in the bunch broke the calm.

At this moment no face stood out before Evan. When nothing more was said, he took a departing step. He was going on if not challenged.

Then a mocking voice called out—"Not runnin', are yuh, Yank?"—and Evan, turning, saw Code Sloan come forward and halt, swaying. Just drunk enough to be wild and doubly dangerous.

"Why would I run?" Evan answered.

"Because of me, by God!"

It was coming, Evan knew. All that wildness. He said: "Why you?"

182

"Yuh're afraid t' face me." Sloan's voice was slurred. He stood with legs braced wide, his pinched face drawn down, his light-colored eyes glittery. A claw-like right hand poised near his gun, tied low on his thigh. Texas gunfighter's stance, Evan reckoned. If this wasn't so deadly serious, Evan had the fleeting thought, it would approach the comical—remindful of a Wild West act. But he jerked himself back to the grim reality of Code Sloan wildly drunk to kill him, and he countered with: "Just what is this? What is this all about? Tell me."

Sloan glared. "Yuh mouthin' around that I tried t' steal yore saddle gun . . . that's what, by God!" He seemed to be working himself up.

"That's not true. You know it isn't."

"Don't call me a liar!"

Empire's crew began to edge away, to get out of the line of fire if Evan drew. Close by, Evan glimpsed Arch Kinder's chiseled face intent on all this.

"I'll put it this way," Evan said steadily. "You've been badly misinformed. Somebody's feeding you tales. Somebody who wants me shot. Somebody's eggin' you on to do it. Maybe somebody's already paid you to do it." He knew instantly the last was the worst accusation he could have made, but it didn't matter now. He was not giving in to this bullying gunfighter.

"That's a lie! Yuh're callin' me a liar! Nobody calls Code Sloan a liar!"

It was coming now, no stopping it. Breaking fast, Evan tensed even more. As ready as he could be.

With a swift, claw-like motion, Sloan dug for his gun, and Evan, as fast, flipped up the cocked carbine and pulled the trigger, his hand jumping with the blast, hearing his weapon a flash before Sloan fired. Evan felt no pain. He levered in another shell, seeing Sloan staggering back, a massive shock filling his face. As Sloan struggled to bring his gun level for another try, Evan shot him again, and levered in another load as Sloan crashed down.

Code Sloan did not get up. No man could take two .52-caliber slugs chest high and regain his feet. Evan tasted powder smoke. Old battle instincts ruled him now. He said not a word. Just watched. Ready, if others took it up.

The scattered crew stood dazed, open-mouthed, their eyes on Sloan in disbelief. One muttered. And another. They couldn't believe it, as if their champion had fallen. Kinder looked on stunned.

When there was more muttering, in it an undercurrent of anger, Logan stepped up beside Evan and called out: "Any more of you *hombres* want into this? If you do, let's get with it now."

Nobody moved toward him. They could only stare at Sloan, twisting and moaning faintly. He still gripped his six-gun.

Keeley, coming out of the store, broke the hanging tension, ordering the crew: "Don't just stand there, you men! Take him to Doc Renshaw's!"

A rider said: "Looks like Code's about done for." Gingerly he took Sloan's gun, glancing at it critically.

With Keeley still urging them on, several men carried Sloan away. Kinder went over to talk to Keeley.

Lucinda waved at Evan from the window and threw him a kiss, but her smile faded to concern when she saw him take the carbine. Why take it going to the store for mail? For the first time she noticed Empire's horses crowding the Gem's hitching rack. Looked like the full crew. Yet logic told her Evan could not have known in advance they would be in town. There had been words between Evan and Code Sloan some time ago, nothing since that she knew. Evan rode armed everywhere he went. Wise, after what had happened on the Emory Pass trail. Wise for any person riding in the mountains, and even along the river, where she would no longer ride alone. So her thoughts ran as she tried to reason away her worry.

She went to her dressing table, her mind on seeing Evan soon. The wait since Wednesday had seemed so long. She sensed that she was smiling, buoyed up by sweet anticipation. She could look ahead with more confidence about everything: the Texas ranch and her holdings in the valley, even about Arch Kinder. And Hap would be here soon.

She was combing her hair when she heard Hannah yelling at her from the steps. "Miss Holloway, come down here! Hurry! Be quick!"

She was there in a twinkling, alarmed at the concern in Hannah's voice. "What is it?"

Hannah led her to the lobby and pointed out the window. "Empire's riders came out of the saloon a minute ago. Now Evan has come out of the store. Dave Logan's behind him." She was speaking in a torrent. "I'm afraid it's a gunfight. That's Code Sloan facing Evan. Bear's pointed him out to me. Evan and Sloan are talking. I don't like this, Lucinda."

Lucinda grasped that and also saw Arch Kinder, standing by like an observer. The same for R.C. Conklin. Why didn't Arch do something? Try to stop this? Code Sloan was a gunman. Evan wasn't. Arch and Conklin and the crew were like an audience waiting for the curtain to go up. Why didn't Arch stop it?

On impulse, she started for the door. Hannah caught her before she could rush outside. "Don't go out there! Be bullets flyin'!"

Both stopped then, and, as they stared across the street,

185

Sloan and Evan seemed locked in position for a moment, broken when Lucinda heard Sloan shout something and claw for his gun and Evan, in a single motion, fire the carbine and Sloan reel backward, firing late. Then Evan shot Sloan again before Sloan could get off a second shot. Now Sloan lay there, twisting and futile, finished. It was over.

There was a momentary pause. The crew staring down at Sloan. Logan seemed to shout a challenge at them, but nobody took it up. Keeley appeared and began shouting at the crew.

Determined, still fearful for Evan, Lucinda flung open the door and ran out, Hannah close behind her. By now Evan had stepped down from the boardwalk to the street, Logan with him.

"Are you all right?" she asked Evan, taking his arm and looking up at him.

He nodded. He seemed to search for words. Slowly coming down from the peak of tautness of only moments ago, he said: "Yes, I'm all right. He got off one shot. I think it was high. I tried to talk him out of it, but he was bent on killing me. I had to defend myself."

Still holding his arm, she could not understand and asked in an astonished way: "But why, Evan, why?"

"A senseless thing. Talk about it later."

He was let down. She saw that. Past the store she could see men carrying Sloan toward the doctor's office. Seeing Kinder talking to Keeley, she felt a surge of anger and went straight over to them.

"Arch," she said, "why didn't you stop this? Why did you let Code Sloan bring this on? Evan said he tried to talk Sloan out of it. Evan had to defend himself." She was pushing at him, her voice accusing and bitter. "I was watching from the hotel. You and Conklin and the riders were like an audience in a theater, waiting for the show to start. You made no effort to stop it. Why?"

"Stop a gunfight?" Kinder threw back. "Don't make me laugh."

"This one . . . yes! Code Sloan is one of your men, and I pay his wages. Now he'll probably die. Evan Shelby could be dead or dying."

"Shelby," Kinder sneered with contempt. "He's been sayin' things around about Code tryin' to steal his saddle gun. Code accused him. It was between them two."

"You could have stopped it."

Evan moved to her side. "You need not bother yourself, Lucinda. This fight was set up. I'm sure of it. For this particular day, when I come in for my mail. A look-out spotted me as I rode up to the hotel. Code Sloan and the crew were waiting when I left the store. Come on," he said, taking her hand.

Kinder said nothing. But if Evan had never seen hate for himself in a man's eyes, he saw it now, smoldering, in Kinder's as he turned her away. Furthermore, what had just happened did not end what lay between Kinder and him.

By now Silas Brown and Bear Webb were there, with Evan and Lucinda and Hannah and Logan, as if to show their loyalty and letting it be known.

"I think," Hannah said distinctly, "it's time for coffee. Come on, everybody."

Little was said for a while as they sipped coffee. It was Logan who asked Evan: "How could you beat a gunman like Code Sloan to the draw with a carbine?"

"Mainly," Evan said, "because I didn't have to reach and draw. I held the carbine at my side. Before I left the store I'd cocked the hammer. When the time came, I flipped it up and fired. It took Code Sloan a split second longer to draw and fire than for me. Otherwise, the ending might have been reversed. Also, the Spencer has a very familiar feel in my hands."

"More than your Colt revolver?"

"Yes. Besides that, I'm slow on the draw. You've seen me practice."

Logan smiled ruefully. "That's what worried me."

Looking first at Lucinda and then around, Evan said: "I want you all to know that I feel no elation about shooting a man. None at all. Just thankful that I could defend myself against a man in a frenzy to kill me."

"But why?" Lucinda asked.

"Hard to say," Evan evaded, letting lie the rumor of money paid Sloan to kill him, avoiding it for her sake as Empire's owner. He saw the same thought fill Logan's face, but the cowman volunteered nothing. "True, Sloan and I had a little tiff when I caught him about to remove my carbine from the saddle. Said he'd just wanted to look at it. We had a few words. Arch Kinder told Sloan to ease off, and I rode on. That was it."

But that wasn't it, Evan saw in her eyes and on the faces of the others. There was more behind it than the saddle-gun tiff. Presently they broke up. Silas and Bear Webb shook Evan's hand, and Evan thanked them and Logan for siding him. Across the way the Gem's hitching rack was empty. Empire had cleared out soon after the shooting. Evan stayed for the noon meal.

When it was time to leave, he said good bye to Lucinda in the office, away from the few restaurant patrons. They kissed and embraced and held each other, lingering.

"It's all right," he said. "Don't worry."

"When will I see you?" she asked.

"I'll come in Sunday. Maybe we can take a little ride."

"Instead, let's just visit here." Her face tightened into sudden concern. "I'm afraid for you now, Evan. I will be whenever you're away from me."

"I can't hide. I'll be on the look-out. Don't worry."

She was not comforted.

He said—"Sunday morning."—and kissed her, waved at Hannah on the way out, and mounted. A grim leftover from the day sent him to the livery and Bear Webb.

"Any word on Code Sloan?" Evan asked.

"He died and went to hell soon after they got 'im to Doc's office. Can't say I'm sorry. Better him than you. Been you, he'd be drunk and braggin' about it at the Gem."

"I had to know."

"That was one helluva shot you made, Cap'n. Code Sloan was a gunslick, all right. I heard an Empire rider say he'd killed nine white men in Texas. Keep a sharp eye out now. No tellin' what else might happen with that Empire bunch still around."

"I will. And you take care of Bear Webb." Evan slapped him on the shoulder. "I appreciate your friendship, Bear."

Traveling down the river road at a running walk, Evan thought he had put the gunfight and its aftereffects behind him. Instead, he found himself carrying the Spencer at the ready, constantly scanning left and right, alert for an ambush. He jerked when a big buck flashed out of the shadows and sprang phantom-like across the road in front of him and vanished magically in the direction of the river.

It occurred to him how much better he would feel if Code Sloan lay wounded back in town. As it was, Evan felt worn down, an old reaction, even though Sloan had been fired up to kill him. He had seen so much killing back in Virginia. After the battle sounds had died, the enveloping, eerie stillness, broken only by the cries and shrieks and haunting prayers of the wounded and the dying. He shook off the feeling and rode on, sensing Arch Kinder was behind the entire matter. Had he paid Sloan? What Dave Logan had picked up at the Gem made sense. No reason for anyone but Kinder to pay Sloan. Why? Because Kinder had big aims in the direction of Empire and Lucinda, and Evan was in the way. Suddenly tired of this damned wariness of what might await him along the road, he reined off it and went through the cottonwoods, splashing across the river, well above the shallows where he usually crossed, and set a course for the cabin.

There was ease here. As Dan took him into the deep stillness of the lower slopes, he caught the distant scent of pines on the wind and Lucinda Holloway's face rose before him, ever fair and loving, and gradually the taut grip of the day's violence fell away, and he knew peace within himself.

After Evan left, Lucinda went to her room, locked the door, and lay down, all at once feeling the weight of everything that had happened catching up and pressing her down. Now Evan had been drawn into her troubles. The very turn of events she had feared most. Only his training had saved him. Arch Kinder could have stopped the gunfight. Why hadn't he? Instinct as true and clear as the tolling of a church bell told her—because he wanted Evan dead. It had all been arranged for Code Sloan to shoot Evan when he rode in. Her fighting spirit returned as it suddenly dawned on her that Evan's life might still be in danger. She could not let this go on much longer.

Just before she felt sleep stealing over her, she prayed silently: *Hurry, Hap. Please hurry. I need you, trusted, beloved old family friend and* compadre *of my father.*

Chapter Sixteen

The arrival of a stage was always of great interest in Rosita, and Hannah Young heard the eastbound from Tucson coming before she saw it bulge with a rush out of the river timber. She paused in her sweeping of the verandah to watch.

A man stepped down, the lone passenger. While Bear Webb hurried up to lead the coach mules away, the man gazed about, showing neither interest nor lack of interest, she thought. At that moment a swirl of wind blew a thin puff of dust toward the stage. After it passed, the man drew a handkerchief from a coat pocket and dusted off his shiny boots. It struck her that he seemed extra proud of his small feet and boots, even vain.

He looked well-dressed for the Mimbres country: dark suit, white shirt and collar with a string tie, a short-brimmed, gray hat. Dark hair hung to his shoulders. A man of medium build. In about his middle forties, she guessed. Of course, a gun belt with the weapon low on his right hip.

From the rear boot of the stage he took one piece of baggage, a long-looking piece; apparently, he was traveling light.

She was behind the counter when he entered. This close, she took in the blade-thin face with the humorless mouth and sandy mustache that drooped and the goatee trimmed to a point and the cool gray eyes that seemed to see all about.

"I should like a room," he informed her in a precise voice.

"You've come to the right place," she said genially. "Dollar a night."

He frowned. "That strikes me as high for this remote area."

"The sheets are clean, and the beds are soft," she said, deciding she did not like this stranger, and she liked most people. "You can rest in peace. No rough stuff allowed."

"I insist that is high," he insisted.

"You don't have to stay here," she replied, holding herself in. "You might ask at the livery, but I don't think they're taking roomers."

His thin lips thinned even more at that. But he said: "I'll stay. I have no choice here."

"It's a dollar in advance per night."

As ungracious as he could be, he took a coin from a pants pocket and flipped it at her. She caught it right-handed, saw it was a twenty-dollar gold piece, and thought: *He figures I can't change it.* If it had hit the floor, she would not have stooped to pick it up, been up to him if he was going to stay here. With a tight rein on her temper, she deliberately counted out nineteen dollars on the counter and said: "Your change, sir. Now your pockets will jingle."

Disgruntled, he began picking up the dollars. When he had put them away, she asked: "Would you like to sign the register, sir?"

He did so with an anger-hard flourish, and she read the bold, slanting words: **Henry Hewitt Birdwell**. He seemed proud of himself.

"We serve three meals a day, Mister Birdwell," she said in an innkeeper's neutral tone of voice. "Twenty-five cents a meal. All you can eat."

"Payable in advance?' He was being sarcastic.

"It's customary to pay after you've eaten." Their little set-to was over, and she said: "Your room is Number Four, sir. Here is your key. Rest well."

Watching him go to the stairs, she wondered: *What in the world could bring that man here? A strange man.* Rosita had been unusually quiet since Evan Shelby had shot Code Sloan in self-defense more than two weeks ago. Any stranger piqued her curiosity. Was Birdwell a businessman with investment plans? She decided he didn't fit the rôle, although he might have the money. Nor was he an order-taker who came to Keeley's store. Nor an itinerant gambler. Whatever he was, she did not feel comfortable around him as she did most men.

Birdwell entered the room and locked it, amused at the simple security. At night he would place a chair against the door. Not that he felt any threat. But the precaution would offer some privacy, an obsession in his hazardous but well-paying, solitary profession.

He removed hat and coat and stroked his long, dark, glossy hair, which he brushed daily. From his baggage he took a small hand mirror and scissors and carefully trimmed his mustache and goatee. That done to his demanding satisfaction, he drew a diamond stickpin from a leather case and held it to the light, reveling in its crystalline beauty. Wishing to avoid appearing as a man of means, he did not wear it in public. In most eyes he hoped he was taken as a mining engineer, a plausible front in New Mexico or Arizona, or as a man interested in small business ventures.

It was now time to practice his training moves, performed daily like a ritual. He squared himself for balance and, right-handed, whipped out the .36 Colt Navy revolver. Reholstering, he drew again and again, until he had performed it ten times. He had another maneuver in which, facing a man, he pretended to shrug and turn away, only to pivot in a flash and fire, catching his opponent unaware. He'd always been incredibly fast with a gun, discovered by accident in a saloon brawl when he was much younger. To him, his sure-handed speed was a gift, and, if you had a gift, he reasoned, you should use it. To his knowledge, no man was faster. Three quick-draw killers of considerable reputation, hoping to add to their reps, had come especially to Tucson to challenge him. And in each face-off duel, Birdwell had shot first with deadly effect, either aiming for the head or the heart. After that, his fame had spread even more. Fear was another factor in his favor, sometimes causing an adversary to tighten up or fumble.

His pliant hands with unusually long fingers called for another step in his exercise. Pouring lotion in the palm of his left hand, he thoroughly massaged his hands down to the tips of his fingers. Then, using a metal clip, he shortened each fingernail.

A .44 Sharps rifle sheathed in his baggage completed his main weaponry. He also carried a double-barreled .41 Remington Derringer secreted deep in a vest pocket, but had no faith in the little banger beyond ten feet. No knives. He was a professional gunman and proud of it. From among his extra clothing he drew out his favorite garment, a mail shirt, composed of small, overlapping rings. He enjoyed the meshing sound of the metal links. The flexible armor, made by an artisan in Mexico City, had saved his life twice, when shot from ambush. Rifle slugs had dented the shirt and bruised his chest. Knowing they had shot him from point-blank range, the exulting ambushers had stood up and revealed themselves. Birdwell had then shot them with ease. One had crawled off into the brush to live long enough to add to his legend of invincibility.

He had shot thirty-three men and one woman for varying fees without serving one day in prison. The beautiful young wife of an elderly California *hacendado* had been lolling in the arms of a virile young *vaquero*. It would not have done for the husband, a man of vast wealth and prestige, to have taken action; word would have leaked out. Birdwell had done it for him at a hefty price, both lovers, making it look like a botched robbery. Too bad all around, people said. Estrella was so beautiful; in fact, beauty had been her downfall. Sad for the old *hacendado* to be left alone in his sundown years. Sometimes life was cruel. And he was such a kind *hacendado*.

. For some years the so-called "moccasin telegraph," the grapevine system of information in the West, had carried whispers about a feared and mysterious killer-for-hire known as Henry Hewitt Birdwell, or H.H. Birdwell, living quietly in Tucson or thereabouts. And there were always powerful men of wealth who wanted others out of the way for various reasons, done so there wasn't the slightest bit of suspicion to themselves, which required a discreet killer. Birdwell had that reputation. The reason didn't matter to him.

Mail addressed to Birdwell at Tucson always went to an obscure little Mexican hotel called El Torro. Birdwell didn't live there. He had a lovely adobe mansion with tiled floors near the Santa Cruz River. A virtual recluse, he was seldom seen about town and had never shot a local person. Bad politics, if he had. Wary Mexicans kept their distance from the unsmiling *gringo*. However, he paid his few servants well. He avoided making friends, thus had no local entanglements. Now and then he'd have a prostitute in.

He had lived in Tucson some time before the residents became aware of him, arriving there after deserting a dying wife and an abused two-year-old son in San Francisco. That was years ago. In his own mind, he knew that his relishing torture and killing of barn cats in his early teens had been a forerunner of what he was to become. For that, his God-fearing father, an Iowa farmer, had literally kicked him out of the house and told him never to return, which he had not and cared not. He cared for no one. Meanwhile, the killings supported his fondness for the physical comforts of life and its finer things.

He never dawdled away time. It was wise to get the business over quickly and be gone, leaving no tracks, so to speak, and few impressions of him to be remembered by individuals. He carried a letter from one Arch Kinder. Big pay. A thousand down, another when finished. He had accepted at once, writing back, liking the travel convenience of only a few hundred miles from Tucson to Rosita.

With a characteristic suddenness, he left and locked the door and went downstairs. When he tipped his hat to the landlady, sitting in her office, she seemed surprised. He must be on his manners now. His complaint about the price of the room had been ill-advised. No more of that. The price was not too high. He was just tight with money.

Heading for the appointed rendezvous, the Gem Saloon, he noticed a few horses out front. The village seemed to drowse, just the way he preferred a place. The fewer people who saw him the better. At the bar he bought a bottle of Old Green River and took it and two shot glasses to a small table toward the rear where he could watch the front.

As the principal player in a deadly game, Birdwell knew men and the dark passions that drove them—vengeance, greed, hate, women, fear of the past. About half an hour later he identified his patron the moment he entered and paused, looking around: the strong, chiseled features, the hint of hidden cruelty in the broad mouth and bold eyes, the powerful build and aggressive stance. The manner of a man who let no obstacle stand in his way.

Birdwell nodded, waiting.

Arch Kinder gave no sign; instead, he went straight to the table and sat.

"I'm Birdwell."

"I'm Kinder."

Each sized up the other without a flicker of change.

Birdwell did not offer his hand, viewing a handshake as a gesture that meant nothing in his profession. Only money was to be trusted.

Pouring two neat drinks and sliding one to Kinder, Birdwell said: "I take it that you have the money?"

"I do. A thousand now, the rest when you finish the job."

"Let me see the first thousand."

"Put your hands under the table."

Birdwell did, and Kinder, from a coat pocket, drew a roll of greenbacks tied with a string and handed it to the gunman, who thrust the roll into a deep front pocket.

"Now," Birdwell asked, "how do I get a look at this particular party?"

"He rides in every other day to see the young woman staying at the hotel, Miss Lucinda Holloway. He lives in a cabin a few miles north of the river ford below town. His name is Evan Shelby."

"Who will point him out to me? I want an eyeball look."

"I will."

The frailties of man often amused Birdwell. He cast Kinder a quizzical look. "This Shelby a suitor of Miss Holloway?"

"You could say that."

"Perhaps a reason behind my mission?"

Kinder sipped his drink, then suddenly downed it. "That is not for you to ask. The man stands in my way . . . is a threat to my entire future."

Almost smiling at Kinder's abrupt unease, Birdwell slowly

emptied his glass and poured for Kinder, then himself. "Reason enough," he said, as if in understanding.

"I am the foreman of Miss Holloway's ranch in Texas. I want it to stay that way."

"You're going to a lot of expense. Why don't you just kill him yourself?"

"I don't want to be anywhere near the killing when it happens. I want to be absolutely in the clear."

"In the eyes of Miss Holloway, at least," Birdwell observed cynically, thinking to himself that any man was an utter fool who let a woman decide his future or tie him down.

"That's what I want."

"At the same time," Birdwell said, "I can't just walk up to this Shelby and gun him down . . . here in town. There'd be a witness or two. A posse . . . if I took off."

"I don't care how you do it, just so you do it."

Birdwell rested his chin on his left hand. "First, there is one precaution I always insist on, which I have had to use more than once . . . that is, keeping a fast horse saddled where I can get to it without delay. After . . . I have collected the rest of my fee."

"Starting tomorrow morning, there will be a saddled horse tied behind the saloon," Kinder readily promised him.

"When will you point Shelby out to me?"

"He hasn't come in today. So he should ride in tomorrow morning. Usually around ten o'clock. First, he will go to the hotel to see Miss Holloway. After that, he may come to the store. If not, you will still get a good look at him."

"From where? The hotel?"

"From a bench in front of the saloon. We will appear to be talkin'."

"Why not the hotel verandah? There are chairs there."

"Too obvious."

Birdwell was scowling. "The way this is shaping up, I may
have to waylay him."

"Ain't that chancy, compared to your speed with a gun?"

Birdwell drew back. "Not a-tall. I am an excellent shot
with a rifle."

"Just so you do it."

"I could trail him when he leaves to go to his cabin. He will
be unaware. His back turned to me. Like cake on a platter, it
will be."

"Just so you do it."

"Then back here, in the saloon, for the pay-off."

"I'll be here with the money."

Chapter Seventeen

Evan Shelby rode into Rosita the next morning and tied up at the hotel, noting more activity than usual this time of day. Bear Webb and Silas Brown were examining a mule, apparently just brought in by a Mexican farmer to sell. Two buggies were pulled up at Doc Renshaw's. The blacksmith shop was clanging away. The saddlery and barbershop looked busy. A clerk at Keeley's was taking groceries out to a wagon. The packed hitching rack at the Gem indicated Empire's crew had arrived in force. Evan wondered how much longer this would go on, knowing Lucinda was anxious to wind up matters.

Arch Kinder and a stranger sat on a bench outside the Gem in earnest conversation. Just now the stranger looked up and appeared to stare in Evan's direction. Evan smiled inwardly. He supposed that he had become a true citizen of the valley since he took notice of every stranger.

He said good morning to Hannah Young, who smiled in a teasing way and said maybe Miss Holloway was in. He rapped on the door marked Number One, spoke his name. Lucinda opened the door and greeted him with a quick kiss and a long embrace.

"You know, this is growing on a man," he said, kissing her on both cheeks and holding her close. She took his hand, and they went to the table and sat across from each other, needing to talk.

"The westbound stage has been running late . . . that means either today or tomorrow," she said with concern. "I do hope Hap McCoy is on it. I had one letter from him. He said his horse fell with him, but he was mending. Promised he'd be here. I know he will."

"He will."

"When he arrives, we'll have a long talk, then I'll call a meeting at the land office and wind up this thing. We have enough pasture now to run a thousand head . . . that's enough. And I shall have fulfilled my father's dream of a ranch in the peaceful Mimbres Valley. I realize now, though he never said so, that he wanted it for me . . . away from the never-ending border violence and watching out for Texas rustlers and Comanche raiders." She looked at him with shining eyes. "Evan, I'm so thankful we've found each other and for the peace you've brought me since my dear father's death."

He held her hand, saying nothing. She needed to talk.

"At the meeting," she said firmly, "after I've told the crew our purpose in the valley has been reached, I will fire Arch Kinder. Not only am I afraid to be alone with him, but I know he hired Code Sloan to kill you. You see, he thinks he can marry me and have Empire, too."

"A word of warning, Lucinda. I want to be there when you call the meeting. Arch Kinder will be furious. You may need Hap and me both. You must let me know ahead of time. Tell Silas or Bear or Keeley to send a man out."

"I know Arch will be furious. But it has to be done. A clean break from the past."

Her oval face was framed in determination. He admired her grit. *Rip Holloway's daughter.*

In thoughtful silence, they watched from the window. The street was stirring. Dave Logan rode up, left his horse in front of Keeley's, and drew hard stares from the Empire crew as he walked without hurry for the store. A rider said something. Logan looked at him, waiting, but the rider made no move, and Logan went on.

"Tension is building up the same way it did that day with Code Sloan," Evan observed. "Men standing around, waiting."

"Waiting for what?" she said.

"For something to happen."

"I can feel it myself. Everything has dragged out too long."

As they watched, Empire's riders entered the Gem except Kinder, who remained seated on a bench with the stranger.

"I wonder who that man is with Arch?" she asked.

"He was there when I rode up," Evan said as a late thought came to him. He said: "I meant to tell you that I have neighbors. A young Mexican by the name of Juan Luna has moved his little family into an old cabin just east of me, across the creek. He rode over yesterday . . . a friendly fellow. I promised I'd help him fix his corral today. He has two mules he needs to keep in. He plans to run a few head of cattle and farm down the river. He's a friend of the Garzas, who will help him get started."

"That makes me very happy . . . and relieved . . . to know that someone will be near," she said, her brows knitting. "I worry about you when you're gone."

Her tone bothered him. "I'll come in early tomorrow morning. You'll stay right here, won't you? You won't ride anywhere?"

"I promise I'll be right here with my good friend, Hannah." She held up a pledging hand.

"If the stage comes in today, you *won't* call the meeting till tomorrow, will you?" He had to make certain.

"Hap and I need to talk over many things first. No meeting till tomorrow, even if the stage comes in today. I promise." She gave him a smile. "We Holloways keep our word."

He smiled back. At the door they held a long embrace and

kissed. He studied her face for another moment, still worried about her and what would happen at the meeting, then went down the stairs.

She waved at him from the window as he turned his horse to take the river road.

"Ain't that sweet?" Arch Kinder sneered. "This is your best chance, Birdwell. Right now. Follow him!"

"I believe it is. I'll take it! Get it done fast."

"Remember, that Henry rifle, on the fast horse I promised, is fully loaded. You can shoot again and again if you miss."

"I don't miss."

"When you've done the job, leave the horse behind the saloon as you found him. Don't ride up in front. I'll be there waiting. I'll see you ride up. Then I'll go through the saloon for the pay-off."

"One more thing," Birdwell said, showing his first signs of nervousness. "I always prefer to leave the vicinity as soon as possible after a mission is completed. How do I get out of here? I don't want to leave my one piece of baggage at the hotel. It has some valuables. If I checked out now, it would create suspicion."

"Simple. Check out in the morning and come to the saloon. As I told you before, a fast horse . . . a different one . . . will be tied out back of the saloon. The old woman at the hotel may wonder, but Shelby's body won't be found for a few days. Meanwhile, you'll be at Fort Bayard, waitin' for the next stage west."

"A sound plan," Birdwell snapped. He got to his feet and rushed through the saloon. Cap Shaw jerked around, looking. What the hell was going on? Arch Kinder and the stranger who drank Old Green River had been in cahoots since yesterday. And what about the saddled horse behind the Gem with the sheathed rifle? An Empire rider had brought the horse in early this morning. Something was about to pop.

Evan was preoccupied as he rode along, his mind traveling back to Lucinda. It had taken a long time to buy up enough range for the ranch, true. Now the anxious waiting for Hap McCoy. If he didn't show up before long, Lucinda would have to act without him, which meant certain trouble with Kinder. He would not take dismissal without a fight. He would take it out on her. She said she feared Kinder, and Kinder would also blame him. Besides himself, Evan thought, there were others who would stand beside her. She absolutely ought not to take action alone. Evan would not let her, brave as she was.

His thoughts were interrupted by the hard beat of a horse behind him? He realized his vigilance, following the Code Sloan shooting, had worn off after everything seemed to quiet down. But, now, he should be more alert again with Lucinda's showdown with Kinder very close. He looked back. Seeing no movement, he put it down to a loose horse running in the river bottom, loose horses he'd seen at times. Wild stuff.

Birdwell followed at a fast trot, just near enough to keep his quarry in sight. It was another episode in an old game to him, stimulating because he always won. Suddenly realizing that he had drawn too close, he reined off into the river timber. He would have preferred a mount easier to control. The rangy bay was fast but high-strung. Now and then it would toss its head, and it noticed every bird taking flight. A rancher like Arch Kinder, used to handling rough stock, would think the bay gentle enough.

Slipping back on the road after a short interval, Birdwell saw Shelby jogging along, obviously in no hurry and not aware. Good. He would make an easy target. But not along here. Someone might happen along the road and witness the killing. It would take place soon after Shelby crossed the river. Birdwell would close the distance and finish it, ride back to the saloon, and collect the rest of his fee. He frowned at the prospects of waiting until tomorrow morning to get out of town. But steady nerves always prevailed in this game, and he needed time to pass before Shelby's body was found, thus the need to kill him across the river.

Coming to the river crossing, Evan halted for his horse to drink. As he rode on, he caught the distant racket of a stage on the river road. Hap McCoy could be on it! Excitement held him. He would ride in to Rosita early tomorrow.

Evan continued to dwell on what it meant for Lucinda to have her father's oldest and most trusted friend at her side, like family, she'd said. And, Evan thought, another gun, if needed.

Again the drumming sound of a horse approaching fast, intruded on his musing. He glanced over his shoulder and saw a dark-suited rider on a bay horse veering in on him. In another swift-closing moment he glimpsed a rifle, and before he could turn away, he felt smashing pain high in his upper left body and heard the blast of the rifle and saw the puff of smoke.

Old battle-trained instincts of survival took over. He whirled his horse away and yanked for the Spencer, eared back the hammer, and fired. Nothing changed. But for a split second his attacker seemed to stare at him, as if surprised Evan was still in the saddle. The range was closing as the other charged, frantic to get off another shot, a wild shot, his horse jumping at the blast.

Hanging low on the right side of his saddle, Evan levered in another round. He fired without visible effect, although sure he was on target. His left arm was of little use other than to help line up the carbine. His attacker was having trouble with his wild-eyed horse, firing and missing.

Evan shot at him again. This time he knew he'd scored a body hit, yet nothing happened. Something was wrong. He had seen the man jerk back a little at the impact, delaying his own shot, tilting his rifle, his shot high. Evan had to get in closer. So he charged with a full-throated yell, a cavalry charge, swerving from side to side, as he heard the frying sound of a bullet.

At eyeball range Evan shot for the head. The rider fell with a cry, dropping his rifle, and toppled from the saddle. One booted foot caught in a stirrup, and the spooky bay horse bolted and ran for the mountains.

A horseman was coming at a run down the slope. He caught the bay's bridle and, after a circling struggle, had the mount in hand, its rider still hung up.

The horseman was Juan Luna, Evan's neighbor.

Evan waved and rode over to him.

"This man . . . tried to kill me," Evan said between gasps.

"I heard the shots, *señor*."

"Thank God, you did."

"Thees man, he looks dead."

"Juan . . . do me a favor. Load him on his saddle. There's a rope there. I'll help. Have to take 'im to town . . . show what happened."

"You don' look like much help, *Señor* Evan. I do it."

Juan Luna was quick and sure with his hands. He found the rifle, a Henry. They started for the river. Evan's left arm hung limply. His shirt was soppy with blood. Suddenly he was beginning to feel quite weak. He hung on. He had to make town.

Lucinda Holloway was in her room going over spending figures and acreage acquisitions from the accounts kept by Keeley. Deep in concentration her mind formed mental images of the locations, above or below Rosita, along the river or into the foothills of the mountains, when Hannah Young called from below: "Lucinda, the stage is coming!"

Lucinda dropped everything and hastened down. She was standing on the verandah when the six-mule stage, swaying, chains rattling, leather slapping, drew up with wheels smoking dust.

She observed as a rotund drummer descended first, loaded down with a case of samples and a thick order book. Then booted feet appeared, feeling for the step, followed by a lean-bodied cowboy dressed for town—neat wide-brimmed gray hat, dark grayish broadcloth pants, blue shirt and—glory be!—a familiar calfskin vest. A gun on his right hip and rifle completed the outfit.

"Hap!" Lucinda yelled, and ran to him. Before he could get out a word, she hugged him hard with her face against the vest, then kissed his grizzled cheek. His slate-gray eyes made her think of her father. "I'm so glad to see you," she told him, tears welling. "How do you feel? Are you all right?"

"Mighty fine," he insisted, embarrassed at all the attention. "Just a little sore."

"And how is Shorty?"

"Roped on 'im just before I left."

"Then he's fine. He's such a good horse."

"I'd shore rather ride him all the way than this swayin', bouncin' mule buggy."

"There's much to tell you," she said, suddenly serious.

His face turned grim. "I've got some things to tell you, too. I've been doin' some back-trackin'. Can't tell you about it here."

He took his grip from the rear boot of the stage, and they walked together to the verandah. Lucinda was worriedly concerned over what the bad news could be. In her mind, all that was bad was here. When she introduced Hap to Hannah, he swept off his hat and bowed graciously, saying: "Mighty pleased to meet you, ma'am."

Hannah held out her hand and exclaimed: "I am pleased to meet you, Mister McCoy, and to have you with us." Inside she said—"You'll be in Number Two, right next to Lucinda in Number One."—and handed him the key. After he signed the register, she said: "Lucinda will tell you we serve ranch-style meals."

"That sounds good to me, ma'am, after the grub I've just had."

From the doorway of the Gem, Arch Kinder witnessed the arrival of the westbound and stared, jaw dropping, when he saw Hap McCoy step down and Lucinda's unrestrained greeting. He glared at them, feeling a distinct unease and a looming threat. What was going on? Why should McCoy pop up here? He'd never liked the older man, and knew that McCoy felt the same toward him, considering him a brash upstart who had impressed Rip Holloway with his tough talk and manner, eager to do anything Rip wanted.

And where was that god-damned Birdwell? He was overdue. Should have been back by now or earlier, the killing done with that new, lever-action Henry rifle, sixteen rounds with one in the chamber. Something must have gone wrong. It took only one shot to knock a man off a horse from behind, then ride up and finish it. Kinder sensed that something had gone wrong.

These thoughts piled through Kinder's mind, growing more and more menacing to his plans. With a sweat of fear, he watched the meeting on the verandah with Hannah Young, watched the three go inside.

A minute or two passed while he brooded. Suddenly he started across the street to the hotel, determined to have it out with them. To defend himself. Empire owed him plenty. He could handle rough men. Had proved it more than once. Over the years hadn't he fought *bandidos* and Comanches for the ranch? Shore, he'd stolen cattle on the side with Code Sloan. Wasn't the only one. Empire was big. Could afford it. Now his whole future hung in the balance. Might say his whole life. He was going to fight for it. Another thought struck, a warning. He'd made a big mistake that day in her room. Lost himself. She was so god-damned pretty. Could drive a man crazy. He'd have taken her right there if she hadn't fought him off. He'd have made her like it, too. Made her beg for more. Brought her down off that finishing-school high horse, by God! Showed her what a real man could do for a woman.

He passed Hannah Young in the lobby without speaking and took the stairs two at a time, boots pounding. She watched him with great dread. What she had feared most seemed about to happen. All coming to a violent conclusion.

Hap and Lucinda went to the room denoted with a Number Two first, where they left Hap's rifle and grip. She said: "We can talk better in my room." Her tension was building.

Not pausing to lock her door, she closed it and turned to him, dreading it but asking: "What is it, Hap?"

He hesitated, avoiding her eyes, then said: "It's about your father . . . all that happened that day. I found out. . . ."

Before he could get it out, boots pounded up to her door, and Arch Kinder jerked it open. He stood fixed in the doorway, on the prod, his eyes like knives. Lucinda shrank back in actual fear. Hap didn't move a hair.

"What's he doin' here?" Kinder demanded, darting a look at Hap.

"I sent for him," she said evenly. "I wanted someone around me I could trust."

"Trust?" Kinder echoed, spreading his hands in pretended hurt, suddenly changing to a placating stance. "After all these years I've rode for Empire, you say that?"

"You are no longer with Empire as foreman and as trail *segundo*. You are fired as of this moment. You are not the same man you once were when Father was alive."

"You can't do this to me!" Kinder's bold features seemed to take on an even harder cast. The blood vessels in his neck stood out like cords. "Your father took me in . . . showed me the ropes . . . made me the youngest *segundo* in Southwest Texas. Now why . . . why are you doing this to me? Why, Lucinda?"

Looking straight at him, her voice never wavering, choosing her words with great care, she said: "I might forgive you for the way you treated me in this room . . . had you ever apologized. But, I guess, Arch Kinder never apologizes."

His eyes were locked on her, an unusual fear deep in them.

"There are other reasons," she said flatly. "I've been going over Empire's books, kept by Mister Keeley. There've been some unusual expenses lately. Only you had access to Empire's pasture account. You drew out hundreds of dollars before Code Sloan tried to kill Evan Shelby. Using my money, you hired Sloan for the job. Why? Because you know I love Evan Shelby."

He started to break in.

"Don't you dare interrupt me! And now, another two thousand dollars are missing from the account . . . money Arch Kinder drew. It's on the books."

"I drew the money out to buy more pasture," Kinder replied, trying to brush it off. "Ask Conklin."

"He left for El Paso a week ago. Besides, we haven't bought pasture for more than two weeks. You're lying! What was it for? To hire another killer?"

Hap McCoy took a step toward Kinder. "I've been backtrackin' you . . . askin' around. We know Rip left the ranch alone that day. He was concerned about cattle being rustled and shoved across the border. What we didn't know then was you came up on him later. You had an argument about cattle."

Kinder threw up his hands in protest. "How can you say that? You're makin' it up to ruin me with Lucinda."

"A little Mexican boy, out lookin' for his stray pony, told me. He saw you ride up to Rip. He heard hot words." A heavy silence had settled over the room. Kinder didn't move. McCoy flicked Lucinda a sympathetic glance, then looked back at Kinder. "He saw you shoot Rip Holloway, the man who had befriended you. Then he saw you kill two Mexican men from his village that happened by . . . on foot to the ranch, lookin' for work. The scared boy hid in the brush till he saw you take Rip's guns and ride off."

Lucinda seemed frozen, feeling a wave of sick dizziness, then the smashing shock of utter clarity and blazing anger and ripping hurt.

McCoy was speaking faster. "So we all thought *bandidos* had shot Rip . . . that he'd shot two of them. That they'd taken his guns. But we couldn't figure out why they'd've left Rip's good cow horse, Hondo? *Bandidos* wouldn't do that. That was a mistake, Arch. You should've shot Hondo or led 'im off somewhere. I found the guns in your quarters . . . buried in the floor."

Lucinda stared at Kinder, shocked by what Hap was saying.

"You can't do this to me!" Kinder shouted, and made a desperate grab for his gun.

McCoy, anticipating, moved faster and shot him twice.

Kinder never got off a shot. The slugs drove him backward. He fell with a crash. Now he wrenched over and with a gasp of vengeful hate snarled at Lucinda: "You'll never see Shelby alive again. I just sent a hired killer after 'im . . . Birdwell . . . the Arizona gunslick!"

Hannah Young heard angry words soon after Arch Kinder had charged up the stairs. She remained attentive, straining to hear once the voices quieted down. After a pause, more words were shouted and then two quick gunshots.

Thinking of Lucinda, she ran up the stairs. Hesitating, fearful of what she'd find, she edged into the room and saw Kinder writhing on the floor, and Hap McCoy standing with drawn gun, and through the gunsmoke Lucinda weeping, hands pressed to her face.

Gritting her teeth, Hannah stepped over Kinder's body and went to Lucinda's side. She put both arms around her. Lucinda looked up and sobbed: "Arch Kinder murdered my father. Hap found out . . . the last thing Arch said to me was that he'd sent a hired killer after Evan a while ago. Birdwell, he said, the Arizona killer."

"Birdwell's registered here. I knew he was up to no good."

"Oh, Hannah, what can I do?"

212

"We'll send men out to Evan's. Now, let's go downstairs."
One arm around Lucinda, Hannah told McCoy: "I'll send
somebody up."

Leaving Lucinda in her office, Hannah ran to the verandah and yelled for help, which was hardly necessary, as
men were already arriving at the hotel.

Evan Shelby heard the two quick shots just as Rosita came
into view. He shook his head, wondering about Lucinda. His
only purpose still was to reach town before he passed out.

Juan Luna rode beside him, leading the bay horse made
skittish by its flopping burden and the smell of blood. At the
sound of the shots, he glanced at Evan, a look of concern
washing over his face.

Evan tried to smile and force a reassuring nod.

Shortly, as they entered town, Evan saw the milling crowd
in the street. Men were running about gathering horses while
Bill Keeley, standing on the boardwalk, appeared to be di-
recting them. Evan urged Dan into a faster pace. Luna kept at
his side.

As they headed down the street toward the crowd, Evan
called out hoarsely: "Where's Arch Kinder? I've got the killer
he sent after me."

The only response from the gathering crowd was a look of
astonishment on each man's face.

Everything was growing dim for Evan as Dan plodded
through the men. One thought left now, only of her, Lucinda.
He swung his leg to dismount and nearly fell. As he staggered,
making his uncertain way toward the hotel, which seemed to
retreat before his eyes, he heard a woman's startled scream.
As Evan tried to focus through the growing dusky light,
Lucinda Holloway's face appeared, not quite in reach, just
before total darkness descended and he knew that he was

falling into a fathomless and faraway place. And from that faraway place he felt the light touch of fingers on his face, and through the sound of heavy weeping he heard his name, repeated over and over, as she called him back.

Chapter Eighteen

The eastbound stage was waiting for Bear Webb to bring out fresh mules. Residents from Rosita and up and down the Mimbres River had come to bid farewell to Lucinda Holloway, departing for Texas with her old family friend, Hap McCoy.

While they waited, visiting as neighbors do, William Keeley said: "Despite her problems with Arch Kinder, Miss Holloway has brought better times to the valley. We've long needed capital. Empire spent freely and paid good money for range land. I know we all hope she will come back before long and make the valley her home."

That drew nods and murmurs of assent.

"She's been mighty friendly and generous," Silas Brown spoke up. "That's because Rip Holloway brought her up right. She's a true ranch girl."

"And to think that Kinder murdered her father," someone said. "What is the story behind that, Mister Keeley? Can you tell me?"

Keeley looked toward the hotel and lowered his voice. "Hannah Young says Rip had caught Kinder rustlin' cattle. Kinder shot him and made it look like bandits had done it. But Hap McCoy found a little Mexican boy who had witnessed the murder. Hap called Kinder's hand on it at the hotel. Both went for their guns. Hap was ready. He shot Kinder twice with a Forty-Five . . . in the chest. Kinder never got off a shot."

"What happened to Empire's crew?" a man asked.

"Miss Holloway paid 'em off right after Kinder was shot.

Scattered to the winds, I'd say. Some to the border, where they'd come from."

"*Señor* Keeley," Pablo Garza said, "we know now Kinder paid Sloan to try to kill our friend, Evan Shelby, then brought in that man called Birdwell . . . from Arizona. But why?"

"Well, it seems Kinder hoped to marry Miss Holloway and control Empire. He wanted to be one of the biggest cowmen in Texas, plus the ranch here. He was a very ambitious man. But when he found out Miss Holloway loved Evan, he tried to have him killed. Evan was in the way of his plans."

"And came near payin' with his life," Dave Logan added. "I heard that Birdwell wore a mail shirt?"

"Yes, he did. Very unusual, but he was a professional killer. That's why Captain Shelby finally had to go for a head shot . . . his last and *only* hope. Fortunately, he's a veteran cavalryman, and he charged Birdwell. Evan told me he thought he'd hit Birdwell. We found the shirt was dented in two places."

"Any idea what Kinder paid Birdwell?" Logan asked.

"We found a thousand dollars on Birdwell. Appears Kinder had paid that down. We also found a letter on Birdwell from Kinder. Birdwell was to get another thousand after he murdered Evan. In fact, Kinder had the second thousand on him when Hap McCoy shot him. All that money has been returned to Empire's account. Sure seems ironic that Kinder was using Miss Holloway's money in an effort to murder the man she loved."

Many among those gathered shook their heads at this information.

"Did Birdwell shoot Evan from the back?" a man asked.

"Tried to, but Evan turned at the last second. Evan was headed for his cabin. Birdwell trailed him. Doc Renshaw says if the bullet had been a few more inches to the left, it would've killed Evan." Keeley paused. "Understand Birdwell was riding a fast but high-strung horse. It's likely that horse joggled his aim a trifle." Keeley smiled. "An Empire horse, too. Whatever, it wasn't Evan's fate to die. We all know Evan's a peaceful man. A peaceful man who was forced to fight two notorious gunmen, and won. In time, all this will become a legend of the valley."

At this juncture Bear Webb led the mules to the stage and, with Silas helping, began hitching up.

Evan Shelby stood watching the crowd gathered around the stage for some minutes from in front of Doc Renshaw's office, after having had another exam. His left arm was in a sling, and his shoulder was heavily bandaged and tied down.

"You're not coughing blood, so the bullet missed your lung," Renshaw had informed him on this visit. "But it tore hell out of other parts. You lost a lot of blood . . . luckily you're in good condition. So take it easy. Rest. Eat a lot. Otherwise, how long's it been now?"

"Eight months," Shelby had replied.

"Fine. I'm proud of you, Evan."

"No sprees and common sense, you know, Doc."

"Now, outta here, Evan!"

It had been a week since Birdwell had shot him. After five days in Renshaw's so-called infirmary, and being fussed over by Lucinda and Hannah, and much coming and going by others, Evan had returned to his cabin.

He and Lucinda had said their painful good byes yesterday evening, but he said he would see her and Hap off today. He felt depressingly low and ineffectual. He would have to find some endeavor to put his all into before long. He'd been considering working out a small-scale cattle deal with Dave Logan. To Evan's mind there was no better man than Dave, whose friendship transcended bitter loyalties of the torn past.

Now he watched as Hap brought Lucinda's baggage to the stage, where the driver took it and loaded it in the rear boot. Lucinda came out on the verandah with Hannah. They spoke a few words, hugged, and wept some, then Lucinda started to the stage.

As she passed through the people of the valley, they spoke what was in their hearts.

"Come back, dear Lucinda."

"You will always be welcome, Lucinda."

"We won't forget you."

A little Mexican girl ran up, curtsied, and presented her with a huge bouquet. Overcome, Lucinda hugged and kissed the little girl. Going slowly on, she waved to everyone and expressed her gratitude, repeatedly. Several women wept while the men looked on somberly.

Through all this, Evan had made his way over to the stage, where he was now waiting. After hugging Josefa Garza, Lucinda turned around to face the stage. She seemed at a loss for words as she looked on at Evan in that touching way she had. Tears glistened in her deep-blue eyes. She smiled. "I may sell Empire," she said uncertainly. "Or I may keep it and have Hap run it."

"Let the dust settle," he said, trying to encourage her with a smile. "Take your time, but hurry back. It will all work out. There'll be much to do."

"A wise man I know well once told me the sun comes up every morning. I'll remember that."

"I'll come if you need me."

"Oh . . . Evan," she whispered, and came to him, the bouquet in one hand. To his surprise, she kissed him fully on the lips, and again and again, then quickly turned away. Hap gave her a hand up into the stage, following her up with a wave at the well-wishers. The stage driver hollered at the restless mules, leather cracked, and they were gone with a surge.

Eight months down, Evan thought, watching the stage grow smaller in the distance. *Four more months until I'm certain.* And he uttered a fervent prayer of thanks and hope.

About the Author

Fred Grove has written extensively in the broad field of Western fiction, from the Civil War and its postwar effect on the expanding West, to modern quarter horse racing in the Southwest. He has received the Western Writers of America Spur Award five times—for his novels COMANCHE CAPTIVES (1961) which also won the Oklahoma Writing Award at the University of Oklahoma and the Levi Strauss Golden Saddleman Award, THE GREAT HORSE RACE (1977), and MATCH RACE (1982), and for his short stories, "Comanche Woman" (1963) and "When the *Caballos* Came" (1968). His novel THE BUFFALO RUNNERS (1968) was chosen for a Western Heritage Award by the National Cowboy Hall of Fame, as was the short story, "Comanche Son" (1961).

He also received a Distinguished Service Award from Western New Mexico University for his regional fiction on the Apache frontier, including the novels PHANTOM WARRIOR (1981) and A FAR TRUMPET (1985). His recent historical novel, BITTER TRUMPET (1989), follows the bittersweet adventures of ex-Confederate Jesse Wilder training Juáristas in Mexico fighting the mercenaries of the Emperor Maximilian. TRAIL OF ROGUES (1993) and MAN ON A RED HORSE (1998) are sequels in this frontier saga.

For a number of years Grove worked on newspapers in Oklahoma and Texas as a sportswriter, straight newsman, and editor. Two of his earlier novels, WARRIOR ROAD (1974) and DRUMS WITHOUT WARRIORS (1976), focus on the brutal Osage murders during the Roaring 'Twenties, a national scandal that brought in the FBI. Of Osage descent, the author grew up in Osage County, Oklahoma during the murders. It was while interviewing Oklahoma pioneers that he became interested in Western fiction. He now resides in Tucson, Arizona, with his wife, Lucile. His next **Five Star Western** will be THE YEARS OF FEAR.

MAY — 2001